FIRE AND FATE IN VEGAS

FIRE AND FATE IN VEGAS

The Accidental Murder of Johnny Ronson

BRIAN WAYNE WEBER

Fire and Fate in Vegas

Interior and cover design by
Caroline Teagle Johnson

Original watercolor "El Rancho in Flames" by
Emely Gonzalez

Printed in the United States of America

GMBL PUBLISHING
ISBN: 978-1-7365324-3-0

First printing

AUTHOR'S NOTE

The El Rancho Vegas resort, and the fire of June 17, 1960 were real, as were Joe W. Brown, Wilbur Clark, Beldon Katleman, Maurice Friedman, Robert O. Schulze, George Harkess, Mrs. P, Howard Hughes, John Battaglia, John Roselli, Joan and Garwood Van, W.E. Leypoldt, Ed Vandenburg, Michael Hines, Ingrid Braecklein, Benny Binion, Benjamin Aronoff, Johnny Tocco, Frank Palermo, Lloyd Armstrong, and Sonny Liston.

The newspaper clippings and quotes contained herein are also real. The celebrities and politicians mentioned are as real as celebrities and politicians ever are. Their appearances are based on historical facts, but any interaction with other characters should be considered fantastical in nature.

The primary plot of this story is fictional. All remaining characters, events, and details are somewhere in between.

"During this era Las Vegas thought of itself as normal; no one else in the United States would have agreed."

—Hal Rothman

PART ONE

CHAPTER ONE

It was the middle of the night, June 17, 1960, and Johnny Ronson was about to stop breathing. He was about to stop doing anything as a matter of fact. Anything that is, except burning to a crisp. Poor Johnny Ronson had the misfortune of being trapped inside a trunk that was inside a truck that was inside the El Rancho Vegas resort... a resort that happened to be burning itself to the ground at the time.

I have a confession to make. No, I didn't kill Johnny Ronson. I'm just the guy who found what was left of him that night, and nearly got myself killed in the process.

My confession is literary rather than criminal.

It seems I have a tendency to start my stories in the middle. I do that because it's usually where the good parts are, but my psychologist says it's a bad habit. People need context first, she says. Otherwise, it's all just random faces and places.

So let me back up a bit. Let's start with the psychologist. Yes, I see one every week, Tuesday mornings at nine. The sessions generally cover whatever situation I've gotten myself mixed up in over the weekend, be it professional or personal in nature. She suggested that we meet on Mondays, but I've rarely resolved any weekend situation by then, so the extra day gives me time to sort things out. And 9 a.m. comes far too early on Mondays anyway.

As fate would have it, June 17th was a Friday, so with the way things were about to play out, my psychologist would definitely be earning her eight dollars and seventy-five cents come the following Tuesday morning.

I should introduce myself. My name is Frank Winston. My friends call me "Wins."

My mother says that's an "ironic misnomer," seeing as how I live in Las Vegas and have never so much as won two bits here... not in any of the local gaming houses downtown, and not in the fancier casino resorts that have cropped up on Highway 91 over the last decade or so. My mother gets along very well with the slot machines of Glitter Gulch, so my lack of gambling prowess has always been a disappointment to her.

I don't win much, I tell her, but then again, I don't play much. A card game now and then to pass the time, maybe shoot dice on a social outing, but I work too hard for my money to willingly hand over much of it to any of the mobsters-cum-businessmen who run this town.

Not that I have anything against those guys. On the contrary, I call a few of them friends, and on the whole, they help keep my business in business. It's just that I prefer to spend my money on martinis and "melanies," which is what I like to call most dames other than my mother and my psychologist these days. That's on account of how my two ex-wives were both named Melanie.

Melanie Boyd was the nice one, the first one, the one I did wrong by with the second one, and the one with whom I still have a surprisingly good rapport. Melanie Rollins was the second one, the impossible to please one, the one I got tied up with too fast for all the wrong reasons, and the one I just as quickly never wanted to see or hear from again.

I have two ex-wives and a psychologist because of my line of work. I'm a private detective... what everyone used to call a "dick." I've been called that several times in my life, and sometimes not as an occupational title. Melanie Rollins called me that a lot during our short-lived wedded bliss. In fairness, I called her a lot of not-so-nice things myself, until I quit calling her at all. These days she is as dead to me as Johnny Ronson.

CHAPTER TWO

The other two melanies in my life both played a part in how I met up with the charred corpse of Johnny Ronson.

First, there's my best girl these days... Amy Loren, 26 years old and the sweetest slice of hot heaven a man could ever hope to spend his time with. Amy has the face of Grace Kelly from when she was doing all those Hitchcock movies, paired with a more voluptuous body that gets points for originality as well as femininity. She's big in all the right places, slim where she needs to be, and I swear parts of her anatomy literally defy gravity.

Amy's fair complexion contrasts perfectly with her brunette locks and her perfectly painted deep auburn lips. She's rarely without the perfect jewelry and the perfect pocketbook to compliment her outfit. I say "perfect" all the time when speaking of Amy because to me she's about as close to perfect as a gal can get. At least as perfect as any I've ever met.

Amy is something of a local girl, born and raised in Pahrump, Nevada, an hour and a half outside of Las Vegas proper, via one of the worst dirt roads you'll ever travel. Her parents moved there from Colorado in the middle of the Great Depression just before Amy was born, and at a time when pretty much no one lived in Pahrump. It's a remote and fairly useless part of the earth to this day in my opinion, except for the fact that it produced the out-of-this-world creature known as Amy Loren. If I ever do marry again, Amy will be the one.

I'm 42 myself, as of two months ago. To save you doing the math, that makes me sixteen years Amy's senior... all but old enough to be her father. Don't think we haven't received our share of grief over that, mostly from otherwise fine folks who concern themselves with such things despite having no vested interest in either of us, or in many cases even knowing us at all. To their credit, her mom and dad are supportive. Amy herself has rarely seemed to even notice the age difference, much less mind it, and far be it from me to complain about that.

I keep myself in shape, so my slightly receding dark hairline gives away my age more than anything else. I get that from my father's side, along with my six-foot-two-inch frame. My blue green eyes are owing to my mother's German ancestry. I dress well of my own accord.

I've been in the P.I. game here since moving to Las Vegas in 1946. What occupied my time before that (beyond the two marriages) is better documented elsewhere, but I will allow that I spent my younger years on the East Coast, in what is still considered by most people there to be more civilized society than the Wild West where I currently reside.

My secretary, Mary Mae Moore, is a Bakersfield, California transplant with an eye for detail, a good level head on her shoulders, three M's in her name, and not one of them a Melanie.

Mae, as she prefers to be called, has worked for me for five years now, which is roughly a year more than I've been with Amy. Mae is 34 and a ginger... plain, but pretty, forgoing heavy makeup in favor of displaying her flawless yet furtively freckled skin.

Mae and I met at an opening party for the Algiers hotel, just after they built it on the east side of the Strip adjacent to the Thunderbird. Fun party, a little too much booze, and Mae and I ended up making it back at my office after... on the very desk from which she now conducts her business for me. Nothing romantic ever came from that night, and the less the lovely Amy knows about it the better... though she doesn't seem to mind when I give Mae a friendly tap on the tush for a job well done. Good secretaries are as rare a commodity as good girlfriends, so I'm careful to keep on the right side of both. Mae is a darn good secretary. She's saved my own less-enticing backside more times than I can remember.

The night of June 17th, Amy and Mae unintentionally conspired to put me in a precarious position at the El Rancho Vegas resort. It all started with a telephone call.

CHAPTER THREE

"Hey boss, I need to tell you something." It was Mae's voice on a house phone at the Stardust, where I was gabbing with my best friend Marty. He's kind of one of those Mafia chums I mentioned before.

The time was a quarter past eight. It had been a long day and I was halfway through my second Mai Tai as we waited to be seated for dinner in the Rapa Nui room at Aku Aku.

I'd been trailing a potentially wayward husband around town at the behest and on the dime of his perennially suspicious wife. It's the type of work I get the least joy from, but it is often the most plentiful and goes a long way toward paying the rent on my small office space, and on my nearby rooms at the Rexford.

It was also pointless work that day. If this husband was cheating, he wasn't doing it on my watch. I'd followed him to the dry cleaner on West Charleston, to a couple shops next to Woolworth's on Fremont Street, and then to the Horseshoe... which appears to have mostly erased Joe W. Brown's name from the place now that he's been dead for more than a year. After losing what looked like a large amount of money there, the husband moved on to the Boulder Club, where he played faro and had two drinks and a cup of coffee... black as far as I could tell. He was always alone, save for me as his shadow.

The Boulder Club was looking much better than the last time I'd been inside, which was a short time after a fire there caused significant damage upstairs... a fire that Johnny Ronson was thankfully 3,000 miles away from at the time. That good fortune bought Johnny about four more years of breathing.

"What is it Mae?" I grumbled, more wearily than I intended.

"Amy telephoned me just now, asking if you can help her friend Jenny find her brother, Johnny. She thinks he's got himself caught up in some kind of trouble tonight."

It was the first time my ears had heard the man's name. "Why didn't Amy just call me herself?"

"Because she didn't know where you are, boss."

That was a fair point. I do a much better job of letting Mae know where I'll be at any specific time of day than I do Amy. Then again, Mae could have just given Amy my location and let her make the call. Doesn't matter I suppose, the result was the same.

"Is this a paying job, or a favor for a friend?" I asked, already knowing the answer.

"I dunno boss, you'd have to ask Amy."

The bartender seemed to be wanting his telephone back. Either that, or he was just nosy. "Okay, thanks Mae. Tell Amy to meet me at the Golden Steer in an hour. I'll start that way now."

"You got it, boss. Be careful."

Mae ended almost every call with "be careful." It was sweet, if often well-nigh impossible to comply with.

That phone call was the extent of Mae's culpability in dragging me into the night's events, but Amy was about to seal the deal.

CHAPTER FOUR

The Golden Steer is my favorite new restaurant in town. It's small, with a bar next to the dining room, and lots of leather and wood throughout. The drinks are generous, the food is delicious, and the prices are fair.

Amy and I go there a lot because she loves their Caesar salad and Chateaubriand almost as much as she loves me... and she loves me plenty. We see a famous face now and then, usually late. Amy got a bit starstruck when she spotted Frank Sinatra in one of the black booths earlier this year. According to the newspapers, he was in town filming a picture, and doing shows in the Copa Room at the time. My namesake is rumored to be a pretty good whiskey drinker if you catch him on the right night. He was drinking a lot of something the night Amy and I were celebrating the anniversary of our going steady. There was a group of what seemed to be friends around him, and I wouldn't let her interrupt with an autograph request, ostensibly out of respect for his privacy. The truth is, I'm not sure I wanted him to get his blue eyes too squarely focused on any part of her... twenty feet away was close enough for my comfort.

I heard later that Jack Kennedy was also in town and hanging out with Sinatra, but if he was there that night I didn't see him. I guess he's likely to be the guy the Democrats pick for President soon, but I haven't been following politics this year. I always vote for the other side anyway. I like Ike, and I can learn to like Nixon too.

That's one subject where Amy and I disagree... politics, so we don't talk much about it. I suspect her support for Mr. Kennedy has little to do with his policies in any event. She frequently tells me how handsome he is, which I guess is supposed to make him qualified to deal with Khrushchev. Come to think of it, I'm glad Mr. Kennedy has never laid eyes on Amy either.

Anyhow, I'm fond of walking when I can, and since Marty had picked me up and wanted to keep the reservation, I decided to walk to the Golden Steer. That was a mistake. I'd forgotten that the temperature was 109 the day before, and if it was more than two degrees cooler when I stepped outside at twilight, I'll be a monkey's uncle.

I noticed the remaining construction activity at the old Royal Nevada site next door as I crossed the bridge then made a left to head north. The Stardust seems to have taken over the space. They called the Royal Nevada the "Showplace of Showtown," and for a time it was exactly that. It didn't last long, but I miss it already.

The dancing waters fountain out in front of the Royal is dry these days, but I wasn't.

I don't sweat much for the most part, but I was soaked by the time I walked past the El Rancho Vegas, not knowing at the time that I might have found and perhaps saved Johnny Ronson if only I'd known to stop and look for him then. Unfortunately for Johnny, I barely knew who I was looking for at that point, let alone where he might be.

CHAPTER FIVE

The sun went down and the mountains slowly disappeared along the horizon as I covered the last half mile between the Stardust and the Golden Steer. I can honestly tell you that I took to this town right away, and I'll never leave... but as I walked, concerns for its future were stuck in my head.

Seeing the new fourteen-story Sahara tower across from the El Rancho had reminded me how fast Las Vegas is growing... maybe too fast. I got here the year before Boulder Dam became Hoover Dam, and ten years after its completion had started to impact the area. The population has tripled since I arrived, and is projected to be more than 60,000 when this year's census is complete. At this rate, we could top 100,000 by the time I'm ready to retire to my rocker. And some days I feel like that day might not be too far away.

Everything is bigger these days. Bigger shows, bigger celebrities, bigger jackpots. Last year at the Desert Inn, I saw Ed Sullivan and Red Skelton come walking up to the clubhouse after a round of golf... with Wilbur Clark in tow. It seems casino managers are becoming better buddies with movie stars and musicians than Bob Hope and Bing Crosby ever were.

Celebrities now come not just to perform, but also to relax and to play. Regular Joes from California and just about everywhere else are doing the same. They built a new convention center to lure even more tourists to town. We already had eight million in 1959, and McCarran Field is getting busier every day. A few of the casinos even have their own airlines now.

More visitors means more hotels, more casinos, and more local residents needed to keep them operating 24 hours a day, 365 days a year. I worry whether there is enough money to go around... the Royal Nevada isn't the only business to fail recently.

More of everything probably means more dough for me, but I'm not sure I like it. I do okay as it is. I've got enough to keep my shoes shined, my shirts starched, and my suits pressed. There's more than enough to keep Amy happy too, though she's grateful for anything, and doesn't ask for much. She made me supper every night for a week after I took her to the new Lido show back at the place I had just left. The show was spectacular, but Amy more so. You should have seen the strapless lilac number she wore that night, or how it looked slipping off her shoulders at her apartment afterward.

I thought too about what I knew about Amy's friend Jenny... the one with the brother named Johnny. It wasn't much.

I knew that Amy had met Jenny at the Day & Nite beauty salon where Jenny worked and where Amy goes to doll herself up. I also knew that they had become friends quickly, and were fond of sunbathing together. Last month, Amy said the two of them caused a stir in the glass pool at the Mirage when they peeked through all seven windows wearing their new bikinis. Knowing Amy, I'm sure they were the itsy bitsy kind, like in that song they still seem to play at least once an hour on KRAM.

I remembered Amy telling me that Jenny is native Hawaiian on her mother's side, with beautifully-tanned skin and dark features. Given that description, I'm not sure why I had never insisted upon meeting the girl.

It had gotten dark, and I was getting hungry. I'd had a decent breakfast, but skipped lunch, and my dinner so far consisted of three or four ounces of sweet spirits, the last portion of which was gulped down as I made my apologies to Marty. I was almost to the restaurant by half past nine, and my mouth was watering more than my overheated forehead.

CHAPTER SIX

"Hiya Frankie," Amy purred as I stepped inside the door at the Golden Steer. I loved the sound of her voice even more than the scent of *L'Heure Bleue* emanating from her ample bosom. She picked up that "Frankie" bit from my mother, by the way.

I gave her a peck on the cheek that was cut short by my realization that a beautifully-tanned half-Hawaiian woman was standing directly behind her.

"This is Jenny," Amy continued, with just a hint of an I-know-you-hate-this-but-you'll-do-it-anyway-because-you-love-me grin starting to form.

I introduced myself to Jenny, and gave her a

friendly hug… my hands taking quick account of her broad shoulders and slender waist. She was a looker, but I kept my look and my hug brief.

I turned to the maitre'd. "Three for dinner, if it's not too late," I requested, but Amy stopped me. "I'm sorry dear, I'm afraid there's no time for a meal tonight. Jenny thinks Johnny could be in a mess right now, so can we please just grab a drink at the bar while she fills you in?"

I brushed the maitre'd aside with my hand and a look of resignation, not sure whether I was feeling more sorry for inconveniencing him, or for the fact that my growling stomach was apparently not going to be sated anytime soon. I wanted a steak, but I got an Old Fashioned.

I ordered Stingers for the ladies, and made a joke about a Polynesian woman interrupting my Polynesian dinner. It fell flat. Jenny was all business, so we jumped right into a quick background on the Ronson siblings.

Jenny and Johnny were twins, and had moved to Las Vegas together the previous year from Honolulu, shortly before the territory became a state. When I asked why they moved from such an enchanting place, Jenny said Johnny was afraid the change in Hawaii's statehood status would impact his parole on a theft rap. I didn't bother trying to sort out the logic or legalities of that, but I did make a mental note that the Ronson brother was an ex-con. That sort tend to find trouble no matter where they land, and usually of their own doing.

I cut to the chase. "Why do you think your brother is in trouble, and why tonight?"

Jenny had a raspy, yet luringly feminine voice... but it was coming out a bit shaky. "I guess it was what he said, or maybe the way he said it, I'm not sure," she began, "plus, I had a premonition this morning, like in The Twilight Zone."

She'd lost me already. "What's a twilight zone?"

"It's a television program," she explained. "It comes on Friday nights on the Columbia network. Ray Bradbury sort of stuff... you know, science fiction."

My eyes rolled reflexively. I was about to put an end to the whole thing right then. I don't work with crazy people. But since I was only two sips into my drink, I decided to ask, "Flying saucers? Martians?"

Her answer didn't reassure me that my decision to continue was a wise one. "Well, there are aliens sometimes," she said, "but this episode was about a military guy who knew which of his friends was going to die."

I played along, for Amy's sake. "How did he know they were going to die?"

"He could see it on their faces, like a vision. I saw that same thing when I looked at Johnny this morning."

I'd had enough. "Okay, I'm gonna need more than a feeling and a fantasy. What did your brother say to you... specifically?"

"He told me thank you for helping him get his life back on the straight and narrow after he got out of jail back home. He told me he didn't mean to let me down, and that he loved me."

I wasn't following. "That sounds nice. I wish my ex-wives had said that last part more often. Doesn't exactly sound ominous."

"The thing is he never talks like that, ever," Jenny insisted. "He's not emotional in that way. I mean, I know he loves me, but he's never told me that before."

I wondered if the maitre'd was still around. Jenny hadn't convinced me yet that anything was urgent or imminent. I gave her one more chance. "Is there anything else?"

"Yes, this. I found it on our kitchen floor right after Johnny left for work. I think he must have dropped it on his way out."

She handed me a piece of slightly crumpled off-white paper. It looked like it had been torn from a hotel stationery pad. I read the handwritten note:

JR —

Meet at my truck late after last drop on Friday. You know where. D says use gloves so no misstakes and stay in uniform so we don't get attention.

Trust me Ray - easy job easy payday.

Now I might be guilty of starting my stories in the middle, but sister Jenny had really buried the lead. She gives me twenty minutes of premonitions and vague expressions of gratitude from a usually stoic sibling, *then* she gets to the "easy payday" note? Contrary to popular belief, there's no such thing as an easy payday in this town.

The note had my attention, and I knew I was taking this job no matter what, on account of Amy, so I asked Jenny if she had any idea who wrote it. She did.

"It has to be his friend Sal," she said, "Sal always calls Johnny 'Ray'... after the singer,

Johnnie Ray. Sal's got a nickname for everybody, except me I guess."

That answer took care of my Ray question too. "Got a last name for Sal?"

"Sal, uh... sorry, I can't remember it. I know it's Italian-sounding, but I just call him 'Sal the Pal.' He's a big guy... very big. Cranky too, but he's nice to me."

I ignored the curious fact that Sal didn't have a nickname for her, but she apparently had one for him. "Who's D?"

"I don't know. Johnny doesn't have any good friends other than Sal."

I pressed Jenny to think harder, and she did. "I guess it could be this guy he sees at the YMCA," she submitted, "David Andrews, or Anders, I'm not sure which. And there's another guy who Sal has been bringing over sometimes. They both just call him Dawson, so maybe he could be D?"

I wasn't sure if she was asking or telling. It's an important distinction. I *asked* her for more specifics as I *told* the bartender to bring me more Dewar's.

"I don't know Dawson very well," was the best she could muster, "but he gives me the creeps. I've only met David once or twice, but he seems sweet. And quiet."

The note suggested that whatever Johnny was involved in was likely job-related, so I moved the conversation in that direction. "Where does your brother work?"

"Not *where*, but *who*," was Jenny's answer. "He works for Beldon Katleman."

I was familiar with the name.

"Sal and Johnny work together," she added.

"Dawson and David too?"

"No. I mean, I'm not sure, but David told me he works part-time at a paint store, and Johnny's never mentioned working with Dawson, so I don't think so."

I asked Jenny what Johnny and Sal did for Beldon Katleman. She said they made deliveries around town, and between Katleman's businesses. Apparently, Johnny typically finished work at midnight, but told her he was working overtime that night and wouldn't be home until morning. She said Johnny always picked up his truck at the Silver Slipper casino at the start of his shifts.

I told Jenny I wanted to keep the note, and asked her if she had a photograph of Johnny. She pulled the wallet from her purse and started to remove a snapshot of the two of them. From the looks of her, it appeared to be from about seven or eight years ago. She was struggling to remove it from the plastic. "You can leave it there," I offered, "just give me a closer look."

I committed the image to memory. Johnny's skin was darker than Jenny's and his hair was longer than most. Big dimple in his chin. I could see that Johnny was only an inch or two taller than Jenny, and she's no more than five-four. They were early to mid-twenties in the photo. If Johnny were a fighter, I'd have put him at a welterweight.

My next question felt like it startled her. "What did your brother steal back in Hawaii?"

Jenny took a sip from her drink. "Ummm... cash, from the register at the store where he worked. I guess he got caught one night with the money from the till in his pocket."

I asked her what type of store, and she took another sip. "Oh... a ukulele shop," she said.

"Did he do much time?"

"Fifteen months in, seven more on probation."

That seemed harsh, but I don't know the court system in Hawaii, so I changed subjects. "Where does Johnny go when he's not at work... besides home?"

"The YMCA mainly, I guess. And he and Sal go to the cinema a lot. I mean, the usual things."

Amy jumped in to ask if I had enough to find Johnny. I told her I had enough to start looking for Johnny. I'd have dug deeper, but I was playing Beat the Clock. Plus, my glass was empty again, so I went with what I had.

I told Jenny I'd see what I could find out and telephone her later. I paid the tab and helped the girls to their feet. They powdered their noses before we left, which gave me time to consider Johnny Ronson's employer.

CHAPTER SEVEN

Beldon Katleman and I have been introduced a few times, but we don't run in the same circles. That's a kind way of saying he knows more Mafia guys than I do. As far as I know, he's not one of them.

I did work for the man once, indirectly, six years ago... when I was still picking up occasional business with my old agency on 5th Street. The El Rancho Vegas was hiring dealers and other casino staff at the time, and I conducted background research on the applicants. That hundred bucks helped pay some bills the summer after I first hung out my own shingle.

The El Rancho is the casino resort that started all of the growth along Highway 91.

There was a smattering of sawdust joints right after the state legalized gambling, which was long before I got here. But it wasn't until 1941 that the El Rancho became the first carpet joint... a nicer place, where a guy can take his girl, and do more than just gamble and drink.

Katleman didn't build the El Rancho Vegas, but he has owned and operated it practically since I've been in town. He also owns part of the New Frontier resort with a man named Maurice Friedman, and a chunk of the Silver Slipper with a guy by the name of Robert O. Schulze. There are others involved too, but it's hard to keep track of them all. I don't know the details of the relationship between the three businesses, but I do know they have employees who are on the payroll of more than one, or at least do work that overlaps between them. I'd just learned that Johnny Ronson and his friend Sal were likely to be two such employees.

Katleman must be my age, maybe a couple years older. He looks older if you ask me, but he might have a different opinion on that. He has one ex-wife, and issues with the current one according to Amy. She thinks he likes weddings more than he likes being married. She's always showing me where the newspaper's talking about somebody tying the knot at the El Rancho... Judy Garland, Steve and Eydie, Paul Newman, I can't remember them all. Personally, I think Katleman just likes to throw parties. He hosted the first atomic test picnic back in 1952, and that started a craze around here. The tourists love the blasts, but I've seen so many by now that I'd much rather watch a good thunderstorm... that's considerably more rare in the Nevada desert.

One thing's for sure, the El Rancho is big on entertainment. Maybe not as much lately, but Katleman gets the top names in the theater. I saw George Gobel there, and Milton Berle too. Amy took me to see Zsa Zsa for my birthday a few years back, and she said Katleman and Zsa Zsa were an item around that time. That might explain some of his issues with the current wife.

Katleman is Jewish, I think, and from somewhere in the midwest originally, though he told me he lived in Los Angeles for a while. He was a military man at one point, and the hair on his head is still cut that way. His chest hair is another story. Every time our paths have crossed, he's been wearing a shirt that revealed enough of that to make Clint Walker jealous.

I knew Katleman had been in his share of dust-ups, but most people in this town have, and I don't pay as much attention to that stuff as some do. I'd never had any personal quarrel with the man, and his check was good.

I'd also heard that the El Rancho's owner is an eccentric, and superstitious to boot. As the valet handed Jenny her keys and I climbed into Amy's Dodge La Femme, I wondered if he had television-inspired premonitions as well.

CHAPTER EIGHT

I drove us back to my place, and Amy came inside while I made a quick change to a less road- weary wardrobe. I dropped the jacket in favor of a white pullover, and slipped into comfortable slacks.

I had Amy pull the phone book from a drawer in my kitchen, in the hope of making short work of the search for D from the note that Jenny had given me. We didn't find any Dawsons, but there were two listings for men named David Andrews and one for a David Anders.

I made some quick calls. The first David Andrews turned out to be deceased since 1951, but his wife still kept the number under his name. She was none too happy about the late night intrusion, and scolded me with words that my mother used to wash my mouth out with soap for. The second David Andrews never worked in a paint store. He also said he hadn't set foot in a YMCA since he took swimming lessons there as a kid.

David Anders turned out to be Johnny's friend, but the roommate who answered the phone said *that* potential D was spending the summer with family in Cleveland. He gave me a number to confirm his story, but it was after 2 a.m. in Ohio... too late to call, lest I offend the sleeping sensibilities of Mr. or Mrs. Anders as I had those of the widow Andrews. Until morning, I had to presume that whoever Dawson was, he was D.

I wanted to make time for a bite to eat, but the daggers shooting from Amy's beautiful browns said that she and my stomach were still at odds. I holstered my Smith & Wesson and walked Amy to her car.

I got in my own vehicle, bound for the Silver Slipper to find out whatever I could about where Johnny had gone after picking up his truck at the start of the night. I drive a red and white Packard Four Hundred... 1956 model, the last year they made them. Far superior to anything Studebaker has come up with.

It crossed my mind that the melanies might be sending me on a wild goose chase. I had little doubt that an ex-con could be up to no good again, but the note was pretty vague, and if something was happening, I didn't have much time to stop it, whatever it was. I motivated myself with wise advice that I picked up from an old Charlie Chan movie. When warned that he was likely engaged in a chase similar to the one I feared, Warner Oland brushed it off with his trademark deadpan, "Have sometimes caught wild goose."

Truth be told, I think Charlie is the one who motivated me into this line of work... though I'm far less witty, and I don't wear hats nearly as well. Hats just slow me down.

It was approaching 11:30 as I zipped down the Strip from the opposite end of where they put up the new sign welcoming everyone to town. By the time you get as far north as I live, you're already committed to whatever it is that fate and luck have in store for you here. The drive to the Slipper was a quick one. There's never much traffic late, when fate and luck seem to be met and made indoors in Las Vegas.

CHAPTER NINE

I've spent quite a bit of time at the Silver Slipper, dating all the way back to when they were calling it the Golden Slipper, and the Silver one was a little hole in the wall with a bar down Boulder Highway. Marty told me that Beldon Katleman bought the original Silver Slipper and closed it down so he could use the name on the current one.

The Slipper has been here in one glistening color or another since 1950. As always, the bright slipper-shaped sign was really lighting up the night sky as I pulled in. I've frequently wondered how the tourists staying nearby can get any sleep. The Desert Inn must have great shades.

When I do gamble, the Silver Slipper is one of the places I play. I have a few connections on the floor, but as late as it was, trying to track Johnny down that way wasn't going to get me the scoop I needed as quickly as I needed it. Plus, if Johnny was in some kind of trouble, for all I knew my connections could be the cause of it.

I drove around back instead, and parked near the commercial loading area. That's where the trucks like Johnny's would pick up or drop off whatever they were carrying, out of sight of all but a handful of the tourists. It's also where the cheap motel rooms would have been if the Silver Slipper Gambling Hall had ever had motel rooms.

There were fourteen or fifteen trucks on-site. I poked around for the better part of an hour and found most of them vacant, no sign of Johnny. I approached one driver who was eating what looked like a liverwurst or bologna sandwich and some cheese, using his dashboard as a dining table. I didn't see a napkin, but he needed one.

I had to speak loudly to be heard over the hum of the still-running engine. "Hey fella, have you seen Johnny Ronson tonight?"

"Who's askin," he managed through a mouthful of orange mush.

I didn't want to tip my hand, so I lied. "I'm a friend of his sister. She's looking for him because their father has taken sick back in Honolulu. Jenny's upset, and wants to talk to him."

The reference to Hawaii and Johnny's twin seemed to sufficiently substantiate my credentials. "I saw Ronson at the start of my shift, and we both dropped off loads next door," the driver offered.

At least I think he said loads. Cheese is difficult to talk through. He could have said they both dropped off *toads* next door for all I know.

"I came back here after," he continued. "I'm not sure where Johnny was headed next. The moss might know."

He probably meant *boss*.

The driver motioned toward a nearby door with his sandwich hand. Through that door

I found no boss. A half-dead fern, but no moss either... just a sign saying "out to lunch." I started to question who eats lunch at that hour, then quickly realized I'd eat just about anything put in front of me... maybe even half a stranger's mystery meat sandwich and some dashboard cheese.

I decided not to wait for the boss. I popped inside the casino to telephone Jenny, to see if she'd heard from Johnny. She hadn't.

The driver's reference to a job "next door" likely meant at the New Frontier... one of those other two casinos that Katleman's involved with. They say it has been around since gambling has been around in this town. It's had a bunch of different names though. I only remember it as the Last Frontier, before they remodeled. The Silver Slipper is on the grounds of the New Frontier's companion old west town (which for some reason is still called the *Last* Frontier Village), so the casinos are very close. Normally, I would have walked there, but I'd had enough exercise on an empty stomach. I climbed back in the Packard, cruised past the Texaco station, and was there in less than three minutes.

CHAPTER TEN

I decided to start inside at the Frontier, because I knew a guy I could trust. It was close to 1 a.m., and the crowd was sparse on the casino floor.

Abe Matthews is a friendly chap, who has worked the overnight shift as the floor manager at the Frontier most every night for the better part of five years. I found him near a 21 table, and he gave me a few minutes of his break time. I didn't recognize him at first, as he'd grown a mustache since the last time I'd been in. One thing hadn't changed… as usual, Abe was in the mood to chat.

"Yeah, I know of Johnny Ronson," he started, "but I don't know too much about him. Johnny works outside and I'm stuck in here the majority of the time. I have had some meetings over at the Slipper lately though, and I've seen him there… talking with the pit bosses, dealers, guys in the cage. He gambles here too sometimes, but I don't think I've ever spoken to him personally beyond daily pleasantries."

I gave Abe the truth regarding why Jenny was worried, and asked him if he'd seen Johnny that night.

"I haven't," Abe replied, "but we did get deliveries earlier, before I started. Chances are he could have been making one of those."

Abe guessed that Johnny was bringing general supplies. "Paper goods, probably," he said, "or it could have been food or liquor if we were short on anything. Nothing perishable. We have an outside service for that, and they come during the day."

I wasn't sure if knowing what was in the deliveries even mattered, so I hadn't asked the driver back at the Silver Slipper. Once Abe brought it up, I realized the contents could be part of any plan I was purportedly trying to prevent.

Abe, eternally the curious type, had a question for me. "What kind of trouble did Ronson's sister mention?" he asked.

"She didn't say exactly," I told him, "just that he was talking strange. And apparently she had a premonition from a television program." I left out the note on purpose, but regretted adding the premonition part even as my mouth formed the words. I regretted it even more when it tripped Abe's chatty switch... the one that quickly drifted, as it tends to do, toward indefinite workplace grievances.

"Television, eh? I got the wife and me a new Admiral set from the Ward's catalog at Christmas. It's got a remote control to change the channel without getting out of my chair... the darndest thing. I listen to Jack Paar before work on the nights that I start late. That is, when he's not getting ticked off and playing hooky like he did this winter. I wish I could talk to *my* bosses like that. You remember that chimp they used to have on the TV in the mornings... Muggsy something or other? He *bit* his boss once. Now that's an idea. Say, what's a television program got to do with Ronson anyway?"

"Probably nothing," was my honest and purposely succinct answer. After that, Abe wanted to talk about the jalopy races at the Sportsdrome, but I had to cut him off. He could shoot the breeze with the best of them, and ordinarily I'd shoot some back, but this wasn't a social call, so I needed to keep moving. I briefly brought up the names of Sal and Dawson, but Abe couldn't help me there.

"I'm gonna have a look outside, if that's okay," I asked, though I was going to do it with or without permission. "Anyone back there I should look for?"

"Bert Engel's the dock guy tonight," Abe answered. "He should be around."

"Got it. I appreciate your time, Abe."

"Sure thing, Wins. Give Amy my best. She's a good gal. Better than you deserve, no offense."

"None taken. You've always been a terrific judge of character, Abe."

CHAPTER ELEVEN

It took me half an hour, but I finally found Bert Engel outside in the parking lot having a Chesterfield. I commented on his brand, hoping to break the ice. It worked.

"If they're good enough for Kirk Douglas, they're good enough for me," Engel proposed. "I sat across from him last year, front table at Dean Martin. He bummed one off me in the can after the show, and he looked healthy enough. We'll both probably live to be 100."

Formal introductions were brief, but I found out Bert Engel was halfway to his longevity goal… about what I'd have guessed, though with bald guys it's hard to tell. Bert said to call him by his first name, which was easy because

I cottoned to him right away.

Maybe it was his shoes. The guy was working outside in all the desert dust, and his two-tone wingtips might have been old, but they were spit polished like he was working the door at Dean Martin, not sitting in the crowd. A man with shoes like that pays attention to detail as a rule, and this one seemed to be no exception.

Bert confirmed that Johnny had been at the Frontier earlier in the evening, then he gave me what I really needed to know... Johnny's last trip of the night was a drop off at the El Rancho Vegas.

I didn't want to press too hard, so I asked a question posed as a comment. "It might help me find him if I knew what he was hauling."

"Decorations. Western-themed stuff. We've got some things we aren't using at the Last Frontier Village anymore, and Beldon's always tinkering with the Rancho's ambiance, so we've been sending stuff over to him there occasionally. Gratis."

"Was it just Johnny, or you had other guys making the run with him?"

"Sal Leonardo went too. They loaded up and left here together a couple hours ago… just before midnight I'd say."

I liked Bert even more now that he'd given me Sal the Pal's last name. He was being generous with information, and not asking why I wanted to know, so I continued. "And when they were done at the El Rancho, what would they do… punch out back at the Slipper?"

"Ronson probably would. He uses a company truck," Bert said. "Leonardo has his own rig, so I'd guess he just went home from there… or wherever else he goes after work. Me, I go straight to my Slumberon. I like to close my eyes before sunup."

Bert was a man after my own heart, but if I was going to be in my own bed anytime soon, I needed to stay focused. I served up more questions.

"Did Johnny and Sal know they'd be working together tonight?"

"Don't know how they could've," Bert said. "I made a change to pencil Leonardo in as the second driver when I got here at eight. His truck is a great deal bigger than our company vehicles, and I thought they'd need the additional room for all that junk."

"Who makes the schedule in the first place?"

"Jim Walters is the main guy here. He works days though, and some of us can make changes if it works out better after he's off."

I asked Bert if he knew whether Johnny or Sal was working overtime. He pursed his lips around the last of the cigarette and flicked it to the ground before answering. We both watched as he stamped out the butt. "Leonardo was on his regular shift until 2 a.m., if I'm not mistaken," he said. "Ronson's off at twelve generally, so yeah he must have been picking up extra time. I don't check schedules that close regarding overtime, and sometimes the drivers swap hours with each other without telling anyone."

"And this man, Leonardo... good guy?"

Bert shrugged. “He’s a big galoot. I swear he goes by Sal because he can’t spell Salvatore without looking at his driver’s license or his u-trou. He’s got a temper that I have to tamp down periodically… the young ones don’t respect authority like they should. But he’s as strong as an ox, and he does his job well.”

“Know anyone by the name of Dawson?”

“No sir.”

My lucky streak with Bert had run out. I peeked at my Timex… it was almost three. Maybe it was just the breezy late spring air, or maybe it was some of that premonition business Johnny’s sister had put in my head earlier, but I was starting to get an eerie feeling inside.

I asked Bert if I could use his telephone. I was headed to the El Rancho, but wanted to speak with Jenny again first. He led me down a service road to his office, and I placed the call. She picked up right away. Still nothing from Johnny. I told Jenny that I thought her brother and Salvatore Leonardo were together as she suspected, and that I was making one more stop to try to find them. I asked Bert to look for a telephone number for Sal in the employee records, but he couldn't find one. I turned down a smoke, shook Bert's hand, and walked back to my car.

CHAPTER TWELVE

I was going to pull up under the new carport at the main casino building of the El Rancho Vegas and leave the car there, but decided to drive around a bit first. I'm not sure what I was looking for exactly, and I wasn't really expecting to see Johnny or Sal. I guess I was hoping something would jump out at me.

Outside the entrance, I saw tourists milling about, workers dumping trash, and a group of casino staff talking to a guy whose gray hair suggested he was a decade older than me... too old to be Sal Leonardo, and not Hawaiian enough to be Johnny Ronson. I also saw two young lovers pitching woo in the grass, three musicians in costume, and a drifter feeding what was either a stray dog or a coyote. Nothing jumped.

I got back on the Strip and drove further north, almost to the corner of San Francisco Street, and turned left to enter from there. I turned left again and parked at the cul-de-sac off Bonita Drive, then gave myself a few minutes to contemplate what I'd learned.

I didn't know for certain who wrote the note to Johnny, but Sal Leonardo seemed like a sure bet. Jenny was convinced it was him, he worked with Johnny, and he had his own truck. Also, I thought Bert Engel was probably joking about Sal's spelling skills, but the note did misspell "misstakes," which would suggest that whoever wrote it wasn't the brightest among us.

I had to make some assumptions. I figured that Johnny and Sal hadn't known they'd be coming to the El Rancho together on their last run, and that Sal's note was to let Johnny know the plan in case they got split up. Since they did get scheduled together at the last minute, I expected to find both of them on the property.

If I was right, Johnny was taking orders from Sal, and they were both taking orders from Dawson, so there were at least those three guys involved. Whether Dawson was taking orders from a fourth guy was a question for a later time... I already had too many guys to search for in the middle of the night.

I realized then that I should have asked Jenny more about what Sal and Dawson looked like. I knew nothing of Dawson's appearance, and all I had on Sal was "big guy, big temper, big truck." That description had been enough to rule out the driver at the Silver Slipper, but not much else. My brain works so much better when it's not being fueled entirely by alcohol and adrenalin.

I had two theories concerning what they could be up to. The first was that they were stealing something from the guests, most likely their automobiles. Johnny had apparently stolen before, but if Jenny was telling me the truth, what he did in Hawaii was small potatoes by comparison. Still, there were numerous vehicles to be had under cover of darkness, and they'd be among the highest value items on the property. I reckoned that the gloves Dawson demanded were in case they couldn't get away with any of the cars they were trying to swipe. He wouldn't want them to leave fingerprints on any steering wheels or door handles.

My second theory was that they were absconding with something that was being delivered to or from the El Rancho. The Mafia has been hijacking delivery trucks and emptying them of their contents since the prohibition days, and while I didn't know if the mob was a part of this, I did know that guys like Johnny and Sal tend to get hired by Mafia guys, or by guys who take their hiring advice from Mafia guys. Johnny, Sal, or more likely Dawson might have had the skinny on something going out the next morning that could already be loaded on a truck… or something already delivered that was waiting to be unloaded. That would certainly be an easy job if you knew where to look, and would explain the late hour of the operation and the benefit to remaining in uniform.

It struck me what a sprawling piece of real estate the El Rancho Vegas had become. The property is enormous… 150 acres easy, with somewhere in the neighborhood of 200 rooms. In addition to a big swimming pool, there's a horse riding area outside, and lots of green grass surrounded by white fencing. Inside, there's a beauty salon and a jewelry shop for the ladies, a men's store, and restaurants and showrooms, both formal and informal. It was all designed to keep guests happy enough that they never had to go anywhere else.

I was at the northeast corner of the property, next to the highway, and near the bungalows that are more like cottages than traditional motel rooms. I had been inside number 505 recently, working a case involving a stolen locket, and the interior wasn't what I expected. It was more New French than Old West… not like they used to be. Since Katleman had previously transformed the Round Up Room into the Opera House theater, I remember thinking that he should probably just put a tower out front and change the name of the place to El Eiffel. Las Vegas is starting to feel like Paris anyway… only with sand instead of the Seine. I guess it's classier than cowboys.

Most of the overnight guests park right in front of where they're staying, so I walked up and down the streets that lead to and from the bungalows. I was scanning for any sign of two or possibly three guys taking too close of a look at someone else's ride. There were a lot of nice automobiles, and one or two that looked like they might not make it past the state line. I stopped to admire a blue 1959 Cadillac with the biggest fins I've ever seen. Any man would be tempted to steal that beauty, but I didn't see anything suspicious going on.

The time was just after four. It would be daylight in a couple hours, but since there wasn't much of a moon, it was still pitch black in many spots, despite the lighted pathways. The temperature had cooled a little, but the southerly wind had picked up. For the ten millionth time in my life, I was glad I wasn't sacrificing the use of one hand to keep a hat in place.

As I was walking west among the bungalows, I had a passing thought that Johnny and Sal could have gotten into the horse thief business. It was a long shot, but the corral wasn't much out of my way up to the casino so I decided to take a look. I didn't see anyone, and the animals were antsy. I like horses, but not when they're in a bad mood, so I didn't stay long.

I doubled back and walked south up Monte Vista Drive toward the main building. My plan was to look for Sal's truck, then some sign of him and Johnny, maybe Dawson. I did that eventually, but not before the Las Vegas landscape changed in an instant.

CHAPTER THIRTEEN

I had just made a right onto El Rancho Drive when I heard a noise that I can't describe well, but I'll try. It was like a piece of timber breaking followed by a sizzle… or like a firecracker fizzing out, but louder. It wasn't jarring exactly, but it cut through the heavy air as clearly as the first rooster's crow at dawn. I looked left, toward the sound, and saw bright orange and blue colors that shouldn't have been there.

Fire! The El Rancho Vegas was burning!

This town has had far more than its share of fires through the years, but nothing on the scale of what I was about to witness. I'd never been caught up in one before, so I had a few seconds where I didn't know what to do. A thousand thoughts ran through my head.

"Does anyone else see this? Where is everybody? They need to get out! Did someone call the fire department? I should help! And… did Johnny Ronson have something to do with this?"

I went with the "I should help!" thought, and started across the lawn diagonally, toward the northeast corner of the building, opposite the main entrance to the casino. It was then that I caught the first wail of approaching fire engines. It was a sound I'll never forget.

I stopped near the shopping corridor as the firemen got to work trying to contain the blaze. It was growing fast, and already starting to engulf large portions of the main building. I knew then that there was going to be very little salvageable by the time this was over. I suspect the firemen did too.

As I walked along the highway side, I could feel the heat for the first time. The fire was increasing in intensity, but there were parts of the building that looked shockingly normal… as if they were completely unaware of what was happening around them. There were people who looked that way too, although in retrospect I think maybe they were just in shock like me. Dumbstruck is the word that comes to mind.

I saw people being helped out by other people, people being rescued by firemen, and people leaving on their own. Surprisingly, I saw people *arriving*. As quickly as the tragedy unfolded, it simultaneously evolved into the greatest show in town. Gamblers and tourists were flocking to the property from who knows where to watch.

There was a lot to see. Those orange and blue colors danced higher and wider with each passing moment. Black smoke billowed upward until it was camouflaged against the still dark sky. There was plenty for the other senses too, with the smell of burning wood as strong as a thousand concurrent campfires, and the crackling flames and frantic conversations competing for attention with a multitude of other indistinguishable, chaotic sounds. The El Rancho Vegas was putting on quite a farewell performance. It was like a one-night-only catastrophic carnival, or a stunningly surreal circus, absent any rings to keep order.

People were moving faster now, more panicked. I looked back behind me and saw guests from the bungalows out of their rooms. Many were carrying heavy wool blankets, presumably to try to help by suffocating the flames, or maybe for protection if the fire shifted their direction. Some people got in their cars, and some had their belongings out on the lawn. There were people sitting, standing, walking, running, driving in every direction. I was helping an older man to the parking lot when we were nearly hit by a black woman driving backwards like a bat out of hell, headed straight for the thickest of the smoke.

I grappled with what to do next. The flames were growing, but the firemen seemed to have rescue efforts under control, and I didn't want to be a hindrance. Should I go back to the car and abandon my night's mission, or should I keep looking for Johnny? If he had been there, I speculated, surely the cops who'd shown up at about the same time as the firemen would have spooked him by now.

I decided to compromise. The delivery trucks were between me and my car, and I could get there around the southwest side of the building, which appeared to be relatively safe. I would take a very quick look for Johnny. If I didn't see him right away, I was done.

Something as unexpected as the fire itself happened on my way there. Half-blinded by the dense smoke and darkness, I ran headlong into a woman. And not just any woman. As I quickly offered my apologies, I saw that I was talking to Betty Grable. Even in that horrible setting, her blue eyes and ruby red lips were instantly recognizable. She was just standing there, several feet from one of the side doors, weeping.

I didn't know what to do, so I embraced her. I assured her everything was going to be okay, even though I was in no way qualified to determine that. She buried her face in my right shoulder, still sobbing.

I held her for what felt like five minutes, but was probably less than one. Then she lifted her gorgeous head, and we separated. "I'm sorry," she managed. "My clothes, my jewelry… where's Harry?" I didn't have much to offer her beyond the shoulder.

Someone she recognized approached, and she started toward him into the murk. As she walked away, she looked back over her own right shoulder. A slight, relieved smile and a half-whispered "thank you" left her lips as she disappeared.

I took a deep breath. A very deep breath. What a strange night it had become.

CHAPTER FOURTEEN

I gathered my wits and moved on. The fire was roaring as I continued down Tutor Way and found a row of delivery trucks. I quickly circled each of them front to back, peeking inside if they were open. Nobody in sight.

When I got to the last truck, I kept moving down the road, toward where I'd left my car. It was getting hard to breathe, even harder to see, and I was going home.

It was then that I noticed the outline of a larger truck, alone, several yards away on the right. It was parked parallel to me, next to the maintenance shop and ice plant behind the main casino building. Flames were close, but my gut said the truck was Sal's, so I had to have a look. I took my pistol in my hand and stepped out into the open area between me and the truck.

Almost immediately, I heard a shot from behind, and felt a bullet fly by my left ear. My heart started pounding like a bass drum as I ducked to the ground on instinct, then quickly picked myself up and made a beeline for the only shelter in sight that wasn't burning… the truck.

There were two more shots as I rolled under the left side of the trailer and crawled on my belly, intending to run into the dark open void on the other side. Except the other side was a wall.

My options were dwindling. I turned right and ran to the back end of the truck, then climbed into the thankfully open cargo space. It wasn't the world's best decision, because I'd trapped myself with only one way out, but it was all I had since the building the truck was parked next to was an inferno.

The light from the fire made it surprisingly

easy to see inside the trailer. I was hoping that whoever was shooting at me didn't see me hop in, but in case he did, I needed a hiding place... preferably a place that provided a little protection and enough room to effectively aim a Smith & Wesson.

The space was virtually empty. Other than loading equipment, the only contents were two large western-looking trunks. They were like something I imagine pioneers would have carried in their covered wagons... or something you'd use to recreate that effect in an old west village. I knew then that I was indeed in Sal Leonardo's truck.

I studied the trunks. They seemed big enough to hold a man, but I wasn't sure they were big enough to hold a six-foot-two-inch man. I decided to find out. The one on my left was larger, so I tried it first. It was fastened tight with two leather straps stretched across the top and buckled in front. When I opened the lid, I found out what kind of trouble Johnny Ronson had been involved in.

The trunk was filled with cash. Loads and loads of paper bills in tight stacks and boxes, and all of it bundled with sleeves marked "El Rancho Vegas."

I had underestimated these guys. They weren't stealing cars or horses, or even hijacking a shipment of goods of some sort. They'd robbed the casino! This was big time... and I was still in big trouble.

I moved to the second trunk. As I looked closer, I saw that it was heavily damaged by fire, and the straps were just laying over the top, unfastened. When I popped the lid, I didn't find money. I found a fully-dead half-Hawaiian twin.

Johnny Ronson had somehow robbed a casino vault of lots of its cash, *and* managed to get himself killed... all in the middle of an out of control fire.

Before I could consider my next move, I felt the floor start to vibrate and heard the engine trying hard to turn over. Somebody was starting the truck.

I appraised the situation. Should I jump back into the line of gunshots and flames, or should I stay put? I chose the latter as we pulled away from the building and started to pick up speed.

My mind was racing faster than the truck. Who was shooting at me, and why? Who was driving, and did he know that dead Johnny and I were his passengers? And where was he taking us?

The truck turned right, and was driving away from the casino building back north toward where my car was parked. I knew that there were two or three corners on the way out where you have to slow down, especially in such a big vehicle.

When we got to the turn onto Hacienda Drive, I leaped out. My right elbow hit the ground hard, but I stood up unscathed, and watched as the truck made its turn and drove off into the barely-emerging sunrise.

Everyone else was watching something different. I turned my head just in time to see the El Rancho Vegas resort's famous wind-mill sign almost entirely engulfed in flames. A moment later, we all gasped as it collapsed and toppled to the ground.

PART TWO

CHAPTER FIFTEEN

It was the middle of the morning, June 21, 1960, and I was still breathing. I was breathing heavily as a matter of fact, as I told the story of the night of the El Rancho Vegas fire to my psychologist. Poor Shirley Carter had the misfortune of being trapped in her chair in her office in pursuit of eight dollars and seventy-five cents… as I struggled to make sense of it all at the time.

"A tin of sardines and a glass of orange juice," I recounted when she inquired as to what I'd eaten when I got home around 6:30 that morning. And in case you're wondering, no, it did not sit well on my stomach. I had slept fitfully for the seven hours or so that followed.

Not that I'm blaming the fish or the fruit entirely. The gunshots likely bore some responsibility. I've been fired at before, but not often, and you never really get used to it. An uncle who was in the war described the aftereffect as the same thing you feel following a near-miss automobile accident, only a hundred times worse. That sounds about right.

There was also the matter of the dead body. It was not my first time seeing one, but you don't really get used to that either... especially when you find them unexpectedly in unexpected places.

I should make one more literary confession.

Johnny Ronson was not completely burned to a crisp... at least not quite as much as I suggested earlier. He *was* most definitely dead. I had very quickly checked for a pulse to verify that, so I knew if he was breathing when he went into either the trunk or the truck, he was not breathing by the time I got to him.

I couldn't rule out any other cause of death, but Johnny's body was burned badly enough to kill him, I have no doubt of that. His hair was gone, but his facial features were intact... even the Cary Grant chin. If he had been completely charred, I don't think I could have been so sure it was him, though the fact that his corpse was wearing a metal nametag that read "Johnny R." did help. They teach you to pick up on clues like that right away at detective school.

Shirley asked how I was doing, and the truth is I wasn't certain. I'd gotten some better food and some better sleep over the weekend, and I'd spoken with my mother by telephone on Monday. That helped, but the unanswered questions still got my goat.

Who was shooting at me? Who was driving the truck? Who was Dawson? Was anyone else involved? How did they get into the vault? How did Johnny end up dead and in the trunk? And was burning down the El Rancho part of the plan?

Shirley's oath required her to keep the details between us, so after I gave her the lowdown on everything that happened, I caught her up on what I'd been doing since Friday.

I had called Amy before going to sleep after the fire, and she went to Jenny's right away to deliver the bad news about Johnny. I joined them both when I woke up early that afternoon.

Jenny was not taking it well. We didn't get into all the details that day, but she did ask me to look into what happened, and I promised I would. I still wasn't going to get paid, but someone shooting at me had made it personal, so I didn't mind as much.

I had also telephoned Cleveland on Saturday to confirm that David Anders, part-time paint store employee, had been in Ohio since mid-May... officially eliminating him from the D derby. Since Johnny Ronson was dead and presumed missing, that left me with Sal Leonardo and Dawson as my only leads. I had to suppose that either Sal or maybe Dawson was driving the truck that I had briefly stowed away in, and that the driver was either the same one of them who was shooting at me, or the other one.

My instincts said a job of such magnitude had at least a fourth guy as well, but he was likely to be high enough up to know not to be seen anywhere near the El Rancho that night... that is unless he had a legitimate reason to do so. Unfortunately, I had absolutely no idea who he might be. And since I didn't have a full name for Dawson, Sal Leonardo was where I had to start.

Mae spoke with the Silver Slipper and the Frontier on Saturday, and found out Sal wasn't scheduled to work on the weekend, and had previously asked for the following week off. There was no Sal Leonardo in my phone directory, so Mae made a trip to the new courthouse on Monday and found his address. I went calling on him there Monday night.

Jenny had told me that Sal was a bachelor, so it surprised me to see that he lived in a house. I found it on Franklin Street... small and boxy, with a low-pitched white rock roof. I also found no one at home, which did not surprise me.

I walked around the property, but Sal's truck wasn't there either. I peeked in three of the windows, and while his place was scant, it didn't look abandoned. My guess was Sal was laying low for a while, but something told me he hadn't left town. That something was the unfinished business related to Johnny's dead body, which I suspected was not part of the plan.

I slipped a business card under Sal's door before I left. I had quickly scribbled an invitation on the back:

I know about ERV, JR, and D.
Let's talk. -FW

I got the initials idea from the "JR" and "D" on the note I was now sure Sal had written to Johnny Ronson. It wasn't that I particularly felt the need to be cryptic, it's just that there isn't a lot of space to write on the back of a business card. I was hoping Sal was bright enough to get the shorthand, and that he was less afraid of me than he was of Dawson or whoever else he might be a liability to.

After I left Sal's, I had stopped at the Cork 'n Bottle for a cheap gin. I drank half of it in bed that night, with very little tonic. I didn't divulge that to Shirley.

CHAPTER SIXTEEN

Amy and I were back at Jenny Ronson's on Tuesday afternoon.

Jenny was still distraught. She wanted to know how and why Johnny died. I didn't have a complete answer to either of those questions. She wondered where Johnny's body might be, and I had to tell her that it was unlikely it would ever be found. I didn't spell it out for her, but I knew that her brother had likely learned the hard way that six feet of desert dirt is the most common early retirement destination for Nevada's wannabe bad guys.

I sensed that Jenny had nothing more to provide regarding Sal Leonardo. I decided to focus on Dawson and anyone else who could have been involved in the heist.

I heard the stutter in her voice again as she spoke Johnny's name, so I tried to be gentle. I asked if Johnny ever discussed other coworkers.

"Nobody by name that I remember," she said. "He complained about all the back and forth between casinos, about too many people giving orders, and about the low pay and late hours, but not about anyone in particular."

"What about Dawson?"

"Like I said before, he came over here a few times with Sal. Johnny just tolerated him. With the age difference, I don't think they had much in common."

Amy and I exchanged a glance. "How old do you think Dawson is?"

"Fifty maybe, or fifty-five. I'm not sure. He's got a lot of gray hair."

"What does he look like, besides the hair?"

"Slobbish, I guess… and scruffy. I mean, he usually had a beer in his hand. His suit never fit quite right. He wore glasses sometimes. I guess he's average height, slightly overweight.

He isn't someone I paid much attention to okay? He always seemed agitated, and I didn't like him."

Jenny seemed a bit agitated herself, and I didn't think I was getting anything useful. "And he's just 'Dawson' as far as you know?"

"Yes," she said. "The first time we were introduced, Sal called him 'Colley' but after that it was always just 'Dawson'."

I thought for a moment. "Maybe his name is Dawson Colley?"

"Could be, I don't know."

I decided to stop there. The ladies continued talking as I excused myself to Johnny's bedroom.

CHAPTER SEVENTEEN

I flipped the switch to illuminate the bare bulb that hung from the middle of the ceiling. Johnny's room was mostly tidy, but not overly so. It had a rustic feel, like part of Polynesia had followed him across the Pacific, except the age of the place suggested that the brown tweed wallpaper had beaten Johnny to the mainland by a quarter of a century.

There was a twin bed in the corner... unmade, with a single pillow. Next to the small window opposite the door was a straight chair that was doing double duty as a magazine rack. I found four issues of Fabulous Las Vegas and six month's worth of Playboys. An issue of the latter near the bottom of the stack had a redhead on the cover and was one I'd seen at the barbershop the last time I was in. I remember reading an article about life in Las Vegas. I hadn't finished it, but what I did read was about sixty percent accurate.

A compact metal desk and a floor lamp were the only other significant furnishings in the room. There was a gold tiki-themed rug covering part of the linoleum floor. The closet was narrow and filled with the usual male accoutrements. Johnny owned too many hats.

I was respectful but thorough when going through the belongings. Johnny's desk and closet yielded nothing of note. It wasn't until I got down on the floor and looked under the bed that I saw anything interesting.

At the head, against the baseboard of the wall with the window, I could see a Cuban cigar box with a rubber band holding the lid in place. I got onto my back and stretched my left arm as far as I could into the corner. I was able to shimmy the box back and forth with my fingertips until I got a good grip and pulled it toward me. Inside the box I found a deck of playing cards, three pairs of dice, and the business calling card of one Robert O. Schulze.

The cards had red backs and looked ordinary, like the kind you'd buy at a five and dime. I inspected the dice closer. One set was from the Silver Slipper casino, and to my eye, they looked normal. The other two pairs were made of a medium dark wood. They were homemade, and clearly worn along the edges… only the wear was too even, which suggested they were shaved intentionally. Guys who cheat at dice do that to make some numbers come up less often, which sweetens the odds in their favor.

The business card gave me pause. Robert Schulze, as I mentioned, is a part owner of the Silver Slipper with Beldon Katleman. The card had "Bob" handwritten on the backside, underneath a different phone number than the one on the front. The DU was the same, but two of the five numbers weren't. The other three numbers were too worn to read.

While it might not be totally unheard of for a delivery driver to have passing contact or even occasional communication with an owner of the casino where he works, it would be quite unusual for him to have the man's personal phone number, and to know him so informally. I tried to convince myself that maybe Johnny just found the card somewhere, or that Robert Schulze and Bob weren't even the same guy... but the proximity of the business card to the other items and the hidden location of the box suggested further investigation was warranted.

I returned to the front room for further investigation.

Amy and Jenny were sharing a bottle of white wine and talking quietly. I interrupted. "Did your brother know Robert Schulze?"

Jenny answered immediately. "I don't know. I don't know who that is."

I tossed out another question... an irrelevant one, to test a theory.

"Did Johnny smoke cigars?"

Another prompt reply. "Yes, sometimes. He likes one... I mean *liked* one after a big meal."

"One more question. Remind me what Johnny was arrested for in Hawaii?"

I hadn't forgotten her answer from back at the Golden Steer, but I wanted to see what Jenny did next. It was exactly what I expected... she took a slow sip of her wine before answering, just as she'd done the first time I asked about Johnny's rap sheet. Jenny Ronson had a tell. She was about to lie to me.

"Stealing. He stole money at work."

I produced the contents of the box, and explained what I knew about the dice. "What should I make of all this?"

Jenny's face gave her away. Seeing those things upset her. She looked down and whispered under her breath. "I thought he'd stopped."

"Stopped what?"

"Illegal gambling."

"Is that what he was actually arrested for?"

No pause this time. "Yes. And it's taken very

seriously in Hawaii. Johnny was arranging craps games at night out of the back of a club where he worked, and the cops found rigged dice when they raided the place."

I had to confront Jenny. "Why did you lie to me before?"

"I don't know. I guess I was trying to protect Johnny. I mean, the gambling arrest is why he was driving a truck for Katleman. Johnny wanted to work on the floor at one of the casinos, but they wouldn't hire him because of his record. He hated that. He was hoping eventually they'd give him a job inside, but they kept telling him they couldn't... not right now anyway. Something about a gambling commission."

Indeed, Johnny's timing had been bad. He'd arrived in town last year at approximately the same time the state's Gaming Control Act went into effect and established the Nevada Gaming Commission. The idea is to keep tighter tabs on casino operators and investors. The stricter regulation is making them all nervous these days, probably until they figure out who to pay off.

I smelled possible motives. "Did Johnny have money trouble, a gambling problem, a grudge against Katleman or anyone else?"

Jenny looked back up at me. "I don't know. He hasn't had rent money the past three months, but I don't know why. I've been covering it for him. Other than that, I just don't know."

His money was going somewhere. "Girlfriend?"

She shook her head no... and then the waterworks started. That always gets me, so I stopped. I told her I'd like to take the box, and she gestured with her hand to indicate that was fine.

It was time for me to go. Amy too. We both had someplace to be.

CHAPTER EIGHTEEN

Before all this happened, Amy and I had planned to get together Tuesday night. We hadn't been out since Helldorado, so despite the circumstances, we decided to keep the date. This case had slowed from its frantic pace, and an evening of distraction would cause no harm. I thought it might even help to clear my head.

We made a pact at the outset to not talk about my work, but before it went into effect, I told Amy that I thought she should have Jenny stay with her for a few days, or have her get a hotel room. I was afraid someone might consider Jenny as much of a loose end as Sal Leonardo.

When the night began, I was in the doghouse with Amy. She'd come over Sunday morning and found my discarded white pullover near the hamper... the pullover that had ruby red lipstick on the collar. Maybelline apparently. Not Amy's color and certainly not her brand... though I have no idea how she knew the latter. I explained my encounter with Betty Grable.

"Yeah, and Elvis Presley and me, we went for an ice cream when he was in town last month. He dumped his whole Memphis Mafia for an afternoon with yours truly." Amy was bad with sarcasm. Showing her a newspaper article confirming that Grable was headlining at the El Rancho the night of the fire helped a bit, but Amy's jealous streak is rarely reasonable.

We ate on Jackson Street, then walked to Town Tavern after. I've been going to Town Tavern since before Amy and I got together. It's a predominantly black club, but recently got new Chinese owners. I think their name is Fong. So far the place is pretty much the same, but they added "New" to the name anyway. It was unusually quiet when we poked our heads in, so we moved on to the Louisiana Club instead.

West Las Vegas has always been more integrated than other areas of town. Most of the businesses there have black owners, but the patrons are of all races. That's different from everywhere else, where until three months ago, blacks weren't even allowed in any of the casinos or hotels unless they were working there or performing. I'd seen exceptions made, but not many.

Amy wondered whether Jenny and Johnny had ever been denied entrance to casinos because of their darker Hawaiian complexions. Probably, I guessed, but noted that she'd never mentioned any difficulty when she and Jenny were prowling the pools. I also reminded her that we agreed not to discuss work. I fully support the desegregation effort and hope it turns out better than things did at the Moulin Rouge, but I can't help thinking that integrating *all* of the resorts could have the unintended consequence of hurting the Westside. Black customers just might start spending their money at the bigger fancier venues.

Amy said she was in the mood for ice cream, and I teased her about still having Elvis Presley on her brain. I suggested the soda fountain at White Cross Drugs, and she agreed.

Not long after we ordered, a chatty young man sat down next to us. We introduced ourselves and he said his name was Wayne. He was husky, but looked to be about 15, so I asked what he was doing out so late alone.

His response caught me off guard. "My brother and I are performing across the street at the Fremont."

The Fremont is one of the newer hotels in town… designed by the same guy who did the El Rancho Vegas. I didn't believe him. "In the showroom?"

"Carnival Lounge. Six sets a night, six nights a week."

The kid was friendly… talked about his

family moving to town a couple years ago, and how he'd won a local talent contest back home. He took off a short time later. We finished our ice cream sodas and decided to walk over and check out his story.

He wasn't lying. We got there just in time to catch the last set of what the sign said were "The Newton Brothers"... music and light comedy. They were terrific. Las Vegas is not usually a town where performers come to *get* famous, but trust me, this kid just might be the exception. He's got charm and charisma in spades.... on stage and off.

We went back to my place after that and Amy slept over. We made love in the morning as the sun came up. I tucked her under the sheets just before I set off for work.

CHAPTER NINETEEN

I generally set my own hours... detective work isn't exactly a nine to five. Still, I'd hoped to be at the office by somewhere close to nine because I had a lot of work to do, and I'd told Mae to expect me.

The big clock outside Gail's bakery said I wasn't gonna make it, but I took time to stop there anyway. As always, I'd smelled the bread about two blocks before I pulled into the parking lot, but that wasn't what lured me in. As much as I enjoy talking with the owner (whose name is George Harkess, not Gail anything) that wasn't my motivation either. I went to Gail's because I needed a bribe. A woman everyone calls "Mrs. P" runs Sammy's newsstand on 2nd Street, across the tracks from the bakery. Sammy's was my next stop, so I grabbed a bag filled with Gail's fresh Famlee loaf to thank Mrs. P for saving the recent out-of-town newspapers for me. Sammy's carries the local dailies, which I'd been reading, plus a bunch from far and wide. I wanted to see what the rest of the country was saying about the fire... and compare it to what the *Sun* and *Review-Journal* were reporting.

Checking the papers was my mother's advice from long ago when I was making my bones in the investigation business. "Pay attention to what people are writing," she said. "Let the reporters do your work for you. That's what they're paid for, and they've got a much bigger budget behind them than you do."

It was good advice. When I talked to her on Monday, she was sticking by it. My mother used to mail me clippings from back East, and now that she lives in Carson City, she promised to do the same with some stories she'd been seeing there.

I got to the office with newspapers in tow at a little after 9:30. Not as late as I expected... I must have made good time at Sammy's. Mae had already brewed coffee. She was wearing a light beige blouse and a darker skirt. Her pumps looked more suited to a night out, but they accented her nyloned legs well. She took a break from organizing my notes on a case at the Glenn Vegas motel, and poured me a cup. "It might be cold, boss," she warned.

She was almost right. I downed the lukewarm concoction while she retrieved Johnny's cigar box from my car. I told her to lock it in her desk drawer. I was meeting my friend Marty again Thursday night and wanted to get his thoughts on its contents before reaching any conclusions.

Over the weekend, I'd learned from the local news that Betty Grable wasn't the only celebrity on the grounds during the El Rancho fire. There were half a dozen other famous folks scattered among the gawking pikers and rounders. I told you they're everywhere these days. It turns out that the woman I saw driving backwards into the smoke was the singer, Pearl Bailey. According to the papers, she crashed her car into a tree... presumably sometime after she almost crashed it into me. And Wilbur Clark's golfing buddy, Red Skelton, had apparently traded his clubs for a camera, and was seen taking photos as the building burned. I'd missed that, but unless he'd inadvertently caught Johnny Ronson being stuffed into a trunk, it wasn't going to help me uncover what was happening behind the scenes that night.

Much of what I found in the out-of-town papers was similar to what I'd been reading locally, but there was new stuff too. There were two things that were consistent in all the stories, and two things that were frequently inconsistent.

The two consistencies were that no fatalities were being reported, and there was no mention of gunshots, theft, or murder. Other than the participants themselves, it was clear I was the only one who knew about those things… except for Amy, Jenny, Shirley, Mae, and my mother of course, and none of them were talking to the newspapers.

What was inconsistent was what was being said about where the fire started and why. Various reports identified the kitchen, the backstage dressing area, and a hallway as the location. Confusion and cloudy memories could explain that, but the conflicting *causes* were more concerning.

In the *Las Vegas Review-Journal's* Sunday paper, it was reported that Beldon Katleman had already identified the source, just one day after the fire.

> El Rancho Vegas owner Beldon Katleman Saturday officially attributed the million-dollar holocaust that razed his hotel in the pre-dawn hours Friday to faulty wiring.

That conclusion sounded more self-serving than official to me, especially in light of what I was seeing in headlines everywhere else.

El Rancho Vegas Destroyed
By Fire: Arson Suspected

ARSON PROBED IN $5 MILLION BLAZE
Fire Levels Las Vegas Hotel

ARSON POSSIBLE?
Costly 'Vegas'
Casino Burns

Why was Katleman so quick to write the fire off to an electrical problem? And why was everyone else suggesting something more sinister? While I was working on that first question, two paragraphs from an Associated Press story answered the second one.

AUTHORITIES were investigating the possibility of arson after being told an unidentified man talked about fire with casino executives three hours before the blaze broke out.

Sheriff's Sgt. Wayne Anderson said deputies are seeking a middle-aged, graying man who had asked casino officials where the hotel's last fire broke out two years ago. That blaze only blackened part of a room.

I wondered… could the middle aged, graying man be Dawson Colley? He fit the description Jenny had given me, and that of the man I saw talking to the casino staff while I was driving around the El Rancho grounds that night. If he talked about fire earlier, it seemed plausible that he could have still been talking about it not long before the fire started. Then again, I didn't get a great look because of the dark, and two thirds of the men in any casino in town would fit that description. Plus, if it was Dawson, why would he have been so carelessly discussing one of the crimes he was planning to commit?

I continued reading for the rest of the morning. The descriptions of the fire made it sound far more orderly than I remembered.

CHAPTER TWENTY

I took Mae to lunch at the Garden Room. It's her favorite. She'd been putting in extra hours, and I was planning to make her come in on the weekend again, so I needed to build up some goodwill. The open-kitchen space at the Sands is airy and relaxing, so we took our time. I had the calf's liver, and Mae went with the ox tongue sandwich, as she always does.

We returned to the office two hours later, and found a note taped to the glass on the front door.

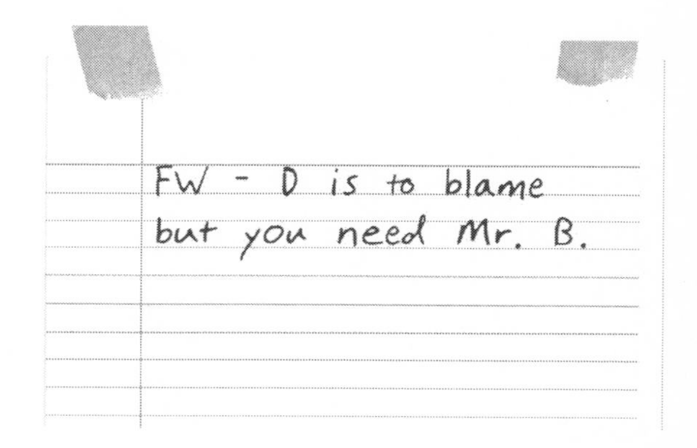

The gambit I'd taken on Sal Leonardo had paid off! I was right that he was scared. There could be no other reason for him to have reached out to me. And I was right that there was a fourth man involved.

Mae interrupted my self-congratulating. "Who's D, boss?"

"A guy named Dawson, I think… or Colley, maybe Dawson Colley," I told her. "Third guy at the El Rancho Vegas the night of the fire if I'm not mistaken." I wasn't sure what D was to blame for, but I suspected shooting at me three times was part of it.

"The name sounds familiar," she said. "Who's

Mr. B?"

"No idea," I admitted, "but whoever he is, it sounds like he's the head honcho."

I gave Mae the chicken scratches from my conversations with Jenny, Abe, Bert, and the driver at the Silver Slipper, and asked her to transcribe them into something coherent. As she sat down at her typewriter, I returned to my desk.

I was happy to have heard from Sal, but was starting to regret the whole initials thing. I surmised that Mr. B referred to either the man's first or last name, as it did with all the other initials Sal and I had both been using in our notes. But with Sal's fondness for nicknames, I couldn't be sure. I went back to the newspapers. This time, I was paying more attention to B than D.

It made sense to start with Beldon Katleman. If they were seriously considering arson, I was sure the police were looking at him too... probably as much as the middle aged, graying man. Faulty wiring or no, as the owner of the

El Rancho, he'd be a natural suspect for torching the place... even to cops who didn't know about the cash that Sal Leonardo, Dawson Colley, and the late Johnny Ronson had seemingly removed just before the fire started.

Katleman wasn't talking about any theft of course, but he was talking about the vault, and the money... as documented in another Associated Press story, and one from Saturday's *Las Vegas Sun*.

* * * *

BELDON KATLEMAN, owner of the resort, estimated the damage at five million dollars.

Katleman also said approximately a half million dollars in cash was in the casino cage and huge vault where the treasury of the plush resort was housed.

Katelman said probably part of the money was lost. The heat prevented him from retrieving it.

* * * *

On hearing earlier reports that the money had not been damaged, Katleman flashed a handful of silver dollars – welded together by flames – and asked:
"Do you think paper money can do any better?"

There were also stories saying Katleman later recovered some bills that were scorched by the flames, but they didn't say he found all of them. The points that stuck in my head were how no one could prove exactly how much money was in the vault, and how easily a fire could cover for any stolen cash. I'm no expert, and it was all speculation, but there were many ways for Katleman to benefit from that uncertainty. His insurance company would likely reimburse at least part of the money, he might be able to claim the losses on his tax return, or maybe he just didn't want to let a fortune sit inside a casino he knew was about to go up in flames.

I leaned back and started to put my feet up. As I did that, I heard Mae exclaim from the other room, "Ray Milland!"

I nearly toppled over. By the time I had

righted myself, Mae was at my door, mimeographed pages flying from both hands. Again, "Ray Milland!"

"What about him?"

"Ray Milland, the actor. He played a guy named Colley Dawson in that picture about the safecracker. It came out around two years ago. You remember Vincent, my boyfriend at the time, God rest his soul? He took me to see it at the Huntridge, boss. Colley Dawson is the guy who got Sal and Johnny into the vault at the El Rancho!"

I told you Mae was good. I gave her a well-deserved tap.

My pride was wounded by the fact that I'd had the name backwards, but I was grateful for Mae's discovery nonetheless. Since Colley Dawson was clearly a nickname, I still didn't know who D was, but I'd definitively placed him at the scene. It was a start.

I switched my attention back to Mr. B, and Mae had a theory on that too...but it was a crazy one.

"Howard Hughes," she called out from her desk, not quite as proudly or as loudly as she'd shouted Ray Milland.

I wasn't so accepting the second time. "Sorry Mae, but there's no 'B' in Howard Hughes' name."

"Yeah, but he's a 'B'illionare!"

That gave me a tickle, but Mae was serious. I reminded her that Mr. Hughes hadn't lived in Las Vegas for more than five years, and even then, only briefly. My money said he'd likely never move back to this town now that he'd settled in Los Angeles. "And why would he have any reason to be involved in what happened at the El Rancho?" I asked. Mae didn't have an answer to that question any more than I did.

I scanned the papers for another hour, then left for the day. I had errands to run, and I felt like a haircut.

CHAPTER TWENTY-ONE

My barber is Gene Papa. Gene also had a theory about Mr. B. He didn't know it was a theory about Mr. B of course, because I hadn't told him about Mr. B or about any of what I was investigating. But Gene, like everyone else, was talking about the El Rancho Vegas fire, and Gene had it in his head that somebody started it on purpose.

"John Battaglia," he said over the buzzing of clippers, and in answer to a question that hadn't been asked. "He's a made man from California, but he's all tangled up with John Roselli and the Chicago Outfit. Roselli was living at the El Rancho until last month when Beldon Katleman tossed him out on his ear.

That fire was payback."

Roselli's name threw me because it sounded so much like Johnny Ronson's, but I kept my story to myself. Gene's conversations are consistently a one-sided affair anyway.

"Battaglia is one of the names in the Black Book," he continued, "and he's none too happy about it either, from what I hear. He can't come anywhere near a casino, and the mob's wanted its paws on the El Rancho for years. Roselli's been trying to make that happen, but Beldon wasn't having it, even though the place is not so *caliente* these days... it's losing money faster than my wife loses my paycheck at the keno parlor. Mark my words, Wins, Katleman's Kastle isn't coming back."

Gene assumed I knew that the Black Book is the list that the new gaming commission came up with... supposedly of guys who are permanently banned from owning, operating, or setting foot inside any casino in town. Truth is, I knew of the list, but hadn't heard it called that before. Luckily, I was lathered up at the time, and six or eight well-timed "mmmhmmms" hid my ignorance.

Gene is from Boston, so as he sharpened his razor, the monologue switched to talk of Ted Williams hitting his 500th homerun over the weekend. Gene said he wished it had come against the Yankees instead of the Indians. If David Anders is a baseball fan, I was thinking he probably felt the same.

I made a note to look into Battaglia as I paid Gene for the shave and trim. The late afternoon sun hurt my eyes as I stepped outside.

I drove down Ogden, and then back north. After inadvertently mixing business with pleasure at Gene's, I was hoping to do that on purpose at Musicland. Garwood Van is the owner of one of the best record shops in town, and he also just happens to have been a former bandleader at the El Rancho Vegas. I thought he might have some thoughts on the fire that could be of help.

He didn't. At least not according to his

wife Joan, who was behind the register when I arrived. "He doesn't know what to think," she said. "He was there in the beginning, and remembers the place being jam-packed from opening night on. He's just very sorry to see it go like that."

I said I'd read that Katelman was planning to rebuild, and had even discussed reopening in a tent, if necessary, during reconstruction. "I hope so," Joan replied, "I used to dance there, you know?"

I nodded, because she'd told me the story many times. In fact, I knew she'd also worked for both the Frontier and the Silver Slipper, which meant she and Johnny Ronson had something in common. Joan and I have something in common too... a love for the game of tennis. Her paper was open to the sports page, and she was lamenting the fact that only four Americans had made it to the third round at Wimbledon. I was lamenting the fact that she didn't seem to have any current knowledge of her former employers.

We turned our attention to music, and I picked out two new albums... one from Julie London, and the other by Bobby Darin. Joan also recommended a recent recording by Miles Davis, and said it was his best yet. I didn't mention it, but even though Melanie Boyd had introduced me to jazz many years earlier, I'd never listened to a Miles Davis LP, much less owned one, so I'd have nothing to compare it to. I took a chance, and she put it in the bag with the others as I handed her a ten.

My last stop was the supermarket. I picked up a six pack of Lucky Lager, a frozen blueberry pie, and a TV dinner... another misnomer, as I planned to pair the Swiss Steak with soothing sounds, not I've Got a Secret.

CHAPTER TWENTY-TWO

I grabbed a churchkey and opened one of the beers as I sat down in the chair opposite my stereo console. My mind was still on Mr. B.

I was looking for a guy with either a connection to the El Rancho Vegas that would have made him want to burn it down, or a reason and opportunity to be involved in stealing its money. A lot of names start with B. Without narrowing down the possibilities by motive and means, even Joe W. Brown, Pearl Bailey, and Bobby Darin could have been suspects if they weren't deceased, female, or at the Copacabana in New York recording a new album at the time. A customer at the record store contributed that last alibi.

I had started to form a list in my head. Beldon Katleman, John Battaglia, and Howard Hughes were on it… though I knew of nothing that would justify the billionaire's inclusion beyond Mae's generally good instincts. There was also Robert "Bob" Schulze, based on the possible connection I'd found between him and Johnny Ronson. It didn't help Schulze's cause that the phone number on the business card in the cigar box was likely private… it didn't match any number I'd been able to find for the Silver Slipper's owner. Bert Engel was on the list too. I had no real motive for him, but he did have a direct connection with Sal and Johnny. And his last-minute schedule change that conveniently placed the two drivers together at the El Rancho the night of the fire made me suspicious, despite the fact that I liked Bert when we spoke.

I also had a new name, based on what I'd read in the newspapers just before leaving the office. W.E. Leypoldt has been sheriff of Clark County since 1955, and has a good reputation.

I haven't met the man, but I have seen him at press conferences and public appearances. I'd never previously had a reason to suspect Leypoldt of any malfeasance, but he is known around town as "Butch," and I'd uncovered a discrepancy in his story concerning the door to the El Rancho's vault.

The *Las Vegas Sun* said a cashier told them that when the fire started he had to crawl to safety on his hands and knees due to the smoke, and that before leaving "he closed the vault door but was too weak to lock it." Wire service stories confirmed that the door was still closed after the fire was out, reporting that fireman had "pried open" the vault with a crowbar while Katleman watched. But Sheriff Leypoldt was quoted in the *Sun* as saying that when he arrived, which was sometime in between the cashier and the firemen, "the door was slightly ajar." Even unlocked doors don't tend to open and close themselves, and discrepancies don't necessarily make men guilty… but they do make me dubious.

The cashier noted in the *Sun* article is a man named Ed Vandenburg. I didn't know him, but I immediately saw him as a suspect... not as a possible Mr. B, because he seemed to be too low level for that. But as a man on the inside with easy access to the vault, I had to consider that Ed Vandenburg could be the man Sal and Johnny called Colley Dawson.

As I put dinner in the oven, I put Bobby Darin on the player. The record was nice. I liked it, and the music fit my mood, but it wasn't as good as the one he had out last year. As I removed the foil from the tray, I realized that Julie London sings like Jenny Ronson speaks... as smoky as the steam rising from my potatoes.

Julie's album was better than the food, but then again it cost four times as much. The lyrics mocked my mediocre meal. "I like my scrambled eggs and bacon served by someone I love," she sang. I don't love anyone named Swanson, but I do love it when Amy cooks for me... especially in the morning, like she sometimes does when I wrap up a case.

I finished the dessert and knocked back another Lucky. It had been a long day, and I drifted off in my chair just after Miles Davis got started. The sound of the needle on the platter woke me long enough to get myself to bed. I'm sure he was good.

CHAPTER TWENTY-THREE

I had to pay the bills on Thursday, so I was back in the legitimate gumshoe business, tracking the potentially wayward husband again. You remember, the one with the perennially suspicious wife?

I followed the man from his home in Henderson to a park, where he sat in the hot sun, and I sat in my hot car, for more than three hours. It looked like he had a lot on his mind, and I could relate. I had enough B's and D's rolling around in my head to make an alphabet soup. By halfway through the stakeout, I'd added one more.

Benny Binion has been accused of just about everything in this town, and convicted of some of it. I'd heard he's back running the Horseshoe from the basement... off the record they say, because the state won't give him a license. I wouldn't be shocked at all if *his* name is in the Black Book. I didn't have means or motive on Binion, but with his reputation and two B's in his name, I figured he'd earned a spot on the list.

I also knew Binion would come in handy in getting me a conversation with Jim Walters. Since Walters is the man that Bert Engel had said did the truck delivery scheduling, I wanted to see if Bert's story about driver changes checked out. I didn't want to ask Walters that directly, so I needed a ruse. An imaginary investigation of Benny Binion wouldn't be much of one because I didn't think there was actually any connection between Walters and Benny, but that was fine because I didn't want to talk about Binion anyway. I just needed a reason to talk to Walters. I could steer the conversation to Bert Engel when I needed to.

In the afternoon, the husband led me

downtown by way of the Strip, taking us past the El Rancho Vegas site on the way. The main building was completely destroyed... reduced to burned pieces of jagged lumber and piles of rubble. The guest rooms and bungalows all appeared to be undamaged. With the casino gone, it was understandable why people had been joking that the El Rancho Motel was now open for business, but it was sad just the same.

When we got to Fremont Street, I thought the husband was en route to a rendezvous at the Sal Sagev, but he stayed on the first floor at the Golden Gate. He wasn't even gambling... he'd just come for lunch. While he was devouring one of their new fifty cent shrimp cocktails, I found a phone and called Jim Walters at the Frontier. He agreed to meet with me there Friday afternoon.

The husband left the casino and walked east past the Pioneer Club, the Lucky Strike, and the Golden Nugget. He peeked in the windows at Bentley's Trading Post, but moved on without going in. What he did next was quite upsetting to his wife when I told her later. As far as I'd seen, her husband didn't have a lover... but he did have a lawyer.

After stepping absent-mindedly in front of a Whittlesea's Blue Cab, the man walked into the Friedman building, and up the stairs to the law office of Michael Hines. I knew Hines as the guy who'd handled the process of getting me matrimonially untangled from Melanie Rollins. Mike wears a white cowboy hat everywhere, and cowboy boots even in the courtroom. He does his job well enough to afford a corner with his name on the windows overlooking Fremont and 3rd, *and* a big ranch with several racehorses not too far from the Strip... which was likely more bad news for my client. Hines invited me to his place once for a party, and let me tell you, it was quite the time.

I left the husband there and drove home to get ready for the evening. Marty and I were seeing a new show at the Tropicana.

CHAPTER TWENTY-FOUR

Martin Grimball and I are the same age, and he's my best friend. At times, he's felt like my only friend. I've always called him "Marty," and he'd probably ask you to do the same. I've known him since the year after I came to town. We get together at least once a week, and we've never had a personal disagreement.

Professionally, he's often a big help. He's from Las Vegas originally, so he's been here since before this town was what it is today. As I said before, Marty is connected, somehow, though I've never inquired further about that than what I wanted to know. It's hard to have many friends in this town without a few of them being tied to one family or another. For that reason, I don't tell Marty all my business, but I do trust him completely with anything I choose to tell him.

Marty is an accountant, with his name on the letterhead at Jones & Grimball. He files my taxes for free. He's shorter than me, and he's got more around the middle. Marty has never married, and he's got a new melanie on his arm every time we're at a social event together. They're invariably easy on the eyes.

It was just the two of us on Thursday night. Marty had been wanting to introduce me to the Tropicana. I try to check out all the new places, but the Tropicana has been open three years, and I'd never been inside... probably because it's so far south. They're working on a golf course next door though, so they must be doing okay.

We saw a show called "Folies Bergere" before dinner. It's a topless show, but with elaborate costuming everywhere else... more of the Paris invasion of Las Vegas. There were seventeen scenes in the production, each more dazzling than the last. Marty counted seventy-five performers on stage, but I think he missed a few. Two honeymooners at our table had just flown in by jet from Phoenix earlier in the day. Marty and I bought them a bottle of champagne, which they shared with the table. The other couple we were seated with had been staying at the Riviera a full week already... about twice as long as most visitors stay anywhere here. They laughed when I said they're practically locals.

Marty and I ate and drank at Perino's afterward, and I showed Marty the dice and cards I'd found in Johnny Ronson's room. Marty's eye is better than mine, and he pointed out where the edges of the Silver Slipper dice had been altered too... just more discreetly than the homemade wood sets. Johnny probably improved his technique in Hawaii's big house. The deck of cards was crooked as well, marked on the backsides so that certain cards could be identified. I would never have noticed that on my own.

I asked Marty if he thought there might be cheating going on at the Silver Slipper.

"Look, Wins, I wouldn't play *bridge* with Beldon Katleman if there was money at stake, and I don't know Robert Schulze well enough to know if he's a straight shooter or not, but I can tell you that they're no dummies," he said. "There has never been a casino shut down for cheating in Las Vegas, and I can't see one of them taking a chance on that right now. Not until things settle down with this gaming commission business."

I saw an opening to pick Marty's brain about Katleman, without giving away what had happened to me at the El Rancho. "Why the distrust of Beldon?"

"I just think he has a side that the public doesn't know, that's all. He comes across as quirky and accommodating, but the guy's in court more than Perry Mason. He's had clashes with the tax service, and gets sued regularly for backing out of business deals or not paying his bills. He even got drug into court on a paternity suit a while back."

"Has he been sued recently?" I asked.

"Don't you read the papers?"

"Only when it involves a case," I admitted, "unless it's on the sports page."

Marty shook his head. "Beldon and a guy named Aronoff... Benjamin Aronoff, have been going at it for a year or more. Aronoff supposedly bought part interest in the El Rancho and never got paid what he was due."

Another B name, but not one I recognized. "Who's Benjamin Aronoff?"

"Old casino guy from way back, from Ohio somewhere."

"Cleveland?"

"Toledo, I think. That's about all I know, except that he usually goes by just 'Ben.' Probably trying to make his move up to the big time here."

Benjamin "Ben" Aronoff was added to my list then and there. I switched subjects to a name I was hoping to remove from the list.

"What do you know about Howard Hughes?"

"Howard Hughes? Why do you want to know about him?"

I don't like lying to Marty, but sometimes it's necessary to mislead him. "I've just been reading about Hughes lately," I said, "and I'm curious what you think."

"Reading? Where? Not in the papers I guess... unless Hughes just signed with the Chargers."

"Very funny," I acknowledged. "Okay, fine, *Mae* has been reading about him, and I just think he's interesting, that's all."

"Well, from what I've been told, he's nine-tenths looney tunes. Gone off the deep end. Bonkers. Tell Mae that what they say in the papers isn't the half of it."

I pressed my luck. "How does he feel about Katleman or Schulze?"

Marty was too clever for me. "Are you investigating Howard Hughes?"

"No!" I lied.

"Hmmm. Well then, I have no idea if Howard Hughes even knows Schulze," Marty started, "but there's history between him and Katleman. Beldon wanted Howard thrown out of the El Rancho years ago because he didn't like the way he was dressed… like a bum. The casino manager wouldn't do it, and ended up out of a job as a result. They might have patched things up since then, or not. Katleman's got history like that with a lot of people."

"Who else?"

"His partner at the Frontier for one… Maury Friedman," Marty replied. "I don't know how they can work together after Katleman punched him in the nose."

"Punched him in the nose? Why?"

"Maybe it was the gut, I don't know. They got into it over a deal they were working on. It happened right in front of their attorneys from what I heard. I'm telling you, Katleman's no saint."

I asked Marty about Ed Vandenburg. I'd found an address and a phone number for Vandenburg, but was hoping for more information before deciding whether to contact him directly. Regrettably, Marty had never heard of the cashier.

We stayed and gambled after dinner, and I lost fourteen dollars. Marty joked that I had a good night at the Tropicana because I lost less than I do when we gamble at the Silver Slipper... and that perhaps they were cheating over there after all. We saw a few of the showgirls on the casino floor greeting customers after the late performance. Marty chatted for a minute or two with one who said her name was Ingrid Braecklein. She was more shapely than some of the girls, with beautiful green eyes and dark hair. She was very sweet, and had a German accent that Marty called "alluring." I couldn't disagree.

CHAPTER TWENTY-FIVE

I sent Mae back to the courthouse on Friday, and I looked through newspapers again, this time on microfilm at the library. It's the kind of background drudgery you never saw Joe Friday do on a Friday or any other day, and I wouldn't be doing it myself if I could afford a secretary *and* an assistant.

Mae and I would have met up later in the day to review what we found, but I had my meeting with Jim Walters that afternoon, so I decided we'd go over everything together on Saturday.

The casino was crowded when I arrived at the Frontier... everyone has full pockets on Fridays. I found Jim's office down a long corridor that was close to where I'd used Bert Engel's phone a week before. Jim started to stand as I entered, but grimaced in pain halfway up. "My lumbago," he explained, extending his right hand from desk level instead. "I don't believe we've had the pleasure."

Jim had a firm grip and he quickly found a friendly smile, partially obscured by a five o'clock shadow that had arrived a few hours early. His black hair was cut in a flat top, and he was wearing a light blue sport coat that fit well but was five years out of fashion.

It felt safe to say that I was investigating Benny Binion on suspicion of gambling-related improprieties. That wouldn't make Jim or anyone else bat an eye. I duped Jim into thinking I'd heard through the grapevine that he might have a connection from Binion's pre-prison days that could be of help to me. As expected, he legitimately denied even knowing the man, beyond what he'd read in the papers. He rightly pointed out that if anyone would know anything about Binion, it would be more likely to be someone on the casino floor or in casino management, not the shipping part of the operation where he works. Jim did offer that the Frontier had faced allegations of cheating some years back, never proven, and said they'd been extra cautious ever since. He doubted anybody there would even take a public meeting with Binion these days as a result.

Jim picked up his pipe and lit the bowl. I could tell he was getting comfortable, so I started steering. "Say Jim, I was here on a different case last week, and happened to meet your guy, Bert Engel. I like him. We had a very nice chat. He struck me as a real gentleman."

"Is that right? Yeah, Bert's a good man," Jim agreed, "and he's done very well here. I hired him myself, must be four years ago now. I'm glad I took a chance on him."

I sensed an opportunity to pry deeper. "Took a chance? How so?"

"Oh, you know, you hear things about guys who come in looking for work... past reputations, family ties, that sort of thing. Bert said he was moving from Chicago because he needed a fresh start."

I revealed that I'd been in that situation myself. "Why did he need a fresh start?"

"I asked him that," Jim said, "and he joked that he was not a fan of the new mayor back there. But that wasn't it. I made a few phone calls, and the real reason was because another Daley had gotten Bert into some shady business dealings in the Windy City... his cousin Calvin."

The pronoun confused me. "Bert's cousin or the mayor's?"

"Bert's. The two of them walked in here together and sat right where you are now... both wanting a job. I passed on the cousin, but Bert seemed to be on the up and up, so I hired him. He's worked out great."

I told Jim I'd never been to Chicago except for Midway, which was true, and then I asked him how he liked casino work. It was a diversion that I then used to transition back to what I was really after. "Does Bert always work nights?"

"He does now, but he didn't until about a year ago. The overnight shift pays more because we have a hard time finding guys who want to be up all night, especially when they have a wife. Bert said he needed the extra money, so he requested the move."

I asked Jim about last-minute scheduling changes like the one that put Johnny Ronson and Sal Leonardo together, but I didn't bring up Johnny or Sal by name, and I didn't say that Bert had made such a change the night of the fire. Jim said switches of that sort are unusual, but they do happen occasionally, and he's fine with it so long as the work gets done well and on time.

We talked for another ten minutes as the smell of Prince Albert filled the small room. When the subject of the El Rancho fire did come up, I stayed mum on anything that wasn't publicly known, but I did manage to slip Ed Vandenburg's name into casual conversation about what I'd seen in the papers. Jim hadn't heard of him either.

I drove by Sal's house again after I left the Frontier. Still no sign of him, but his guppies weren't belly up yet, so I figured he must be stopping by. I considered leaving another note, but I knew if he wanted to talk more, he'd do it on his own time.

CHAPTER TWENTY-SIX

Many years ago, Marty introduced me to a man named Johnny Tocco. Tocco had just converted an old mob hangout into a boxing gym, and Marty got us in to watch some of the local up-and-coming fighters hone their skills. Marty only went once... he didn't care for the heat or the smell of the place, but Tocco's been letting me stop by from time to time ever since.

I went to the gym on Saturday morning, correctly anticipating that a few of Tocco's old business associates might be there too. I was hoping to catch any chatter about someone who might be known as Mr. B, and I thought for a while that I'd caught some.

There was a lot of talk among the regulars about a mobbed-up manager called Frank Palermo. He goes by "Blinky." It was a B nickname, but it was a false alarm. It turned out the talk was all related to the government being in Blinky's face about the connection between boxing and organized crime. Nothing about the El Rancho.

A trainer named Lloyd Armstrong kept the morning from being a total loss. I didn't find Mr. B, and I didn't even see Blinky, but because I stuck around an extra hour as Armstrong suggested, I did see Blinky and Tocco's top contender. You might have heard of Sonny Liston. He's a heavyweight who's already fought three times this year, and he's got another match coming up soon. I watched him spar a couple rounds, then take a turn on the bag. With hands like his, Sonny could spot Katleman a punch or two and still knock him out in the first round.

I made my way to the office by mid-afternoon. Mae arrived a short time later, her hair up in curlers.

I razzed her a bit. "Date night?"

"Mind your own beeswax, boss."

She smirked, and I did as I was told. We got down to business, comparing our research on the eight potential Mr. B's. Even without Blinky Palermo, the list had expanded by one, with Marty unwittingly adding Ben Aronoff to the roster of Beldon Katleman, Bert Engel, Butch Leypoldt, Bob Schulze, John Battaglia, Benny Binion, and Howard Hughes.

We started with Bert. I hadn't found anything at the library the day before, but Mae discovered court records showing that he had financial troubles back in Chicago... he'd been declared insolvent in 1955 under the Bankruptcy Act. I assumed that was as a result of the shady business dealings Jim Walters had spoken of. Bert's shift change at the Frontier suggested that he might still be having money problems. That didn't make Bert a thief, but I supposed it did give him motive for taking a few greenbacks from a casino vault. And even though Jim wasn't concerned about Bert changing the driver assignments after hours, I was. I knew Bert was scheduled to be back at work on Monday night, and decided to talk to him again then.

Despite Marty's telling of Howard Hughes' history with Katleman, a minor disagreement over bad clothing choices was a weak motive for either arson or theft, let alone murder. Then again, with Hughes' purported mental state, any perceived slight could be enough of one. And with his money, he had the means to do just about anything. Mae was excited to report that she'd discovered Hughes does have a B in his name, right in the middle of his middle name, "Robard." I discounted that as a longshot source of any nickname, if for no other reason than I doubted Sal Leonardo knew how to spell Robard.

I wasn't sure what to make of the crooked cards and dice. With what I knew, and after talking to Marty, it was clear to me that Johnny Ronson was up to something besides what happened at the El Rancho. I considered that maybe that was what got him killed. But why would someone take him out while also stealing money from a resort and possibly burning it down? The cigar box alone wasn't sufficient to connect Bob Schulze to Johnny, and neither of us had found any allegations of cheating at the Silver Slipper. There was also nothing of note between Schulze and either the El Rancho Vegas or Beldon Katleman.

Benjamin Aronoff was, in fact, from Toledo, and had been in the gambling business there since the thirties. He was said to have a good reputation. He had been arrested though… because gambling is illegal in Ohio. I'd run out of time before finding much more than that about Aronoff, and the only thing Mae found on him in Nevada was the lawsuit with Katleman that Marty brought up at dinner.

The court records showed that Aronoff claimed to have purchased 49% of the El Rancho for half a million dollars. If I'm not mistaken, that's almost exactly what it cost to build the entire place twenty years ago. Things apparently went south between Aronoff and Katleman in a hurry, and they'd been fighting over profits, expectations, and power ever since. Aronoff even got the El Rancho closed down briefly last year… an occurrence I had evidently missed in the papers. Both men were throwing numbers at a judge about who owed who what. It looked like they'd worked out an arrangement at some point, but according to the most recent records that Mae found, there was still a court case pending between them.

I didn't come up with any motive for John Battaglia and John Roselli, or anything connecting them to each other. John Battaglia's interests were primarily in Los Angeles. He'd been arrested in Las Vegas in February, but the charges were minor… vagrancy and speeding. That might give him a beef with Butch Leypoldt, but not with Katleman or the El Rancho. John Roselli did have dealings with a *Sam* Battaglia who was connected to the Chicago Outfit, and who had recently been held in contempt for his testimony to Congress.

Unfortunately, I couldn't find anything to show that the two Battaglias are even related. I decided maybe my barber had bungled them. I did find that both Battaglias have colorful nicknames…"Johnny *the Bat*" and "Sammy *teets*." That didn't help me at all, but I imagined Sal Leonardo would find it amusing.

I'd also dug into Maurice Friedman. I didn't see anything about the confrontation with Katleman that Marty talked about, but I did find an extensive arrest record, and connections to names that make Benny Binion look like a choir boy. There was no B in his name, but with all the nicknames floating in the air, I put him down as another potential suspect.

We quit just before sundown, and I walked home. I don't know where Mae went.

CHAPTER TWENTY-SEVEN

I telephoned Amy right after Bonanza, and was happy to hear that Jenny was staying at Amy's place as I'd suggested. Amy was doing her best to keep Jenny distracted. They'd been clothes shopping at Fanny's and Kathleen O'Nee that morning, before having a late lunch at Foxy's. They were about to go bowling when I called. Amy said she missed me, and I told her the same. I gave Jenny an update that was very short on details.

I hung up, and had just stepped in the shower when the telephone rang again. I thought Amy must have forgotten to tell me something, so I jumped out. I nearly fell on the bathroom floor as I reached for a towel, but I got to the phone in time… pride and tailbone intact. It wasn't Amy on the other end.

"Hello."

"Hi Frank, It's Jim Walters… from the Frontier. I'm sorry to bother you at home so late, and on a weekend, but I'm afraid I have some bad news."

I hate when someone says that. "What is it Jim?"

"I'm calling because we spoke about Bert Engel at length yesterday, and I could tell you were quite fond of him."

I said that was true. But then again I barely knew the man.

"He's dead, Frank. Bert's wife found him in the garage this morning, with the engine still running. It looks like suicide."

I felt a tingle go up my spine. I had no words… so Jim continued. "Listen Frank, I don't know how important Engel was to whatever you were investigating over here, but I thought you'd like to know."

He paused, then added, "It's a terrible tragedy."

I agreed. I thanked Jim for the call and put down the receiver.

I found some words, but they were all profane. I needed to think, so I swapped the shower for a long hot soak in the tub. The rest of the night was a blur.

CHAPTER TWENTY-EIGHT

I woke up Sunday morning with a headache. More like three headaches. I still didn't know where Sal Leonardo was, I still didn't know who D was, and one of my potential Mr. B's… the only one I had hoped didn't do it, was dead.

I am as suspicious of suspected suicides as I am of faultless fires, so I wondered whether Bert Engel's money woes were bad enough that he decided to go for the big sleep instead of his usual one after work. Or was he feeling guilty for his part in a heist that had gone awry and become a murder too? Of course there was also the possibility that Bert had been removed by someone higher up to guarantee his silence… a fifth man. I didn't want to think about that, or about the unsettling fact that my conversation with Jim Walters happened just a few hours before Bert's premature demise.

I telephoned Mae and asked her to meet me at the office at one o'clock. She complained, but she complied. We spent the afternoon and early part of the evening reviewing what we knew.

Not long after dark, I stood up to stretch my legs. I was just starting to pour myself a scotch when I heard the front door open. I looked up to see an enormous man standing at the entryway between Mae's space and mine. He was at least two inches taller than me, and he easily had me by a hundred pounds. As he stepped forward, Mae appeared from behind with her Rolodex poised to clock him. I reached for my gun, but neither of us would need our weapon.... Sal Leonardo was about to voluntarily hand us his head. All that was missing was a silver platter.

Sal grabbed a chair and took a seat without

one being offered. "I killed Johnny Ronson!" he boomed.

I sat back down very slowly, keeping my eyes on him the whole time. Mae stepped away and stood in the corner, nervously biting at her lip. I noticed that Sal was nervous too. "Why are you telling me this?" I asked.

His voice remained too loud. "Because I'd rather be in the slammer than in the ground!"

Sal pulled a Polaroid from his pocket and slid it across my desk with a hand that was burned and had three bandaged fingers. The photograph showed a dead man who looked to be 50 years old, 55 perhaps. His eyes were open, but the bullet hole between his graying eyebrows confirmed his deadness. I asked a second question that I was quite sure I knew the answer to. "Who is this?"

I expected him to say Colley Dawson, or maybe Ed Vandenburg. He didn't. He said "Calvin Daley."

I couldn't hide my shock. "Bert Engel's cousin?"

"Whose cousin?"

"Bert Engel's," I repeated. "I assume he's Mr. B... from your note?"

"I didn't know Bert Engel had a cousin," Sal said, "and I don't know who Mr. B is. Only D knew that, and this is D... Calvin Daley!"

Sal was supposed to be dumb, but I was the one who was falling behind. "I thought D was the guy you call Colley, or Dawson, Colley Dawson."

"Same guy," Sal said. "He hated that nickname."

I wanted to make sure I had it straight. "So Calvin Daley is Colley Dawson, and he's the guy who got you into the vault at the El Rancho Vegas?"

Sal swore under his breath. He seemed surprised that I was playing catch up. "Yes! Your note said you knew about D. I thought someone had you stick the picture of him under my door to send me another message."

I slid something back across my desk at Sal... the note he'd written to Johnny. "I knew about D being involved, but I didn't know who he was. And I didn't leave any picture... just the one note." I explained. "Who did this to him?"

"I don't know. Mr. B, probably. That's why I'm here!"

"You're afraid you're next?"

"I am next!"

I didn't dare tell Sal that Bert was dead too... I needed him to relax. "Was Calvin Daley the guy who was shooting at me?"

"I didn't know who he was shooting at," he said. "I thought it might be me. I was trying to get the hell out of there anyway, so when I heard gunshots, I took off."

"In your truck?"

"Yeah."

I informed Sal that I was riding in the back as he hightailed it from the El Rancho. I ordered him to tell me exactly what happened that night, and he gave me a concerned look. "Are you gonna arrest me?" he asked.

"I can't arrest you, I'm not a cop."

"Turn me in, then?"

"Just talk, Sal... no promises."

He didn't hesitate further. "Okay, so we started taking the money from the vault around 3:30…"

"Hold on. Start at the beginning," I demanded. "You left the Frontier around midnight. What then?"

"We unloaded at the El Rancho."

"So the delivery of western decorations was legitimate?"

"We brought the stuff to the El Rancho and dropped it off there, if that's what you mean."

It was what I meant, but his answer didn't prove the delivery wasn't cover. "Did you know you'd be working with Johnny that night and making the late delivery to the El Rancho together?"

"No. They never tell us beforehand," Sal said. "That's why I left the note for Johnny on Wednesday when I got word from Daley that the job was on for Friday. Daley gave me the two trunks that night at the Frontier."

"Gave you the trunks *which* night at the Frontier… Wednesday or Friday?"

"Wednesday."

Sal's answer meant that he had what he needed to secure the money regardless of whether he got scheduled to the El Rancho on Friday or not. I asked him if he knew why Bert added him at the last minute, and he said Bert didn't give him a reason. I knew that there were two possible reasons. One was the reason Bert gave me... big truck for a big load. The other possible reason was to make sure both Johnny and Sal made it to the El Rancho that night, and didn't get sidetracked or hung up somewhere else. Sadly, I didn't know which reason was the real one, and Bert was no longer in a position to talk.

"Okay, so Daley found you at 3:30 the night of the fire?"

"No," Sal said. "He *found* us around 2:00, as he'd told me he would. At 2:00, he said we needed to wait until the vault was open, and that he'd come back and let us know when to begin. He did *that* at 3:30."

I was having trouble finding my footing.

"Did Daley crack the safe himself, or did someone leave it open for him?"

"No idea. He just said we would find it open. And we did."

"It looked like a lot of money, Sal. How much did Daley tell you to take?"

"Three hundred thousand. Thirty for me and Johnny to split, another thirty for Daley, and $240,000 for Mr. B. Two trunks full."

"One trunk was full of Johnny Ronson," I shot back. It probably sounded callous, but then again, I was talking to the man who had just admitted to killing Johnny, so I wasn't trying to be kind.

Sal took a breath and sat back in his chair. I thought I sensed remorse. I told him to continue.

"We filled up the big trunk with $200,000 and loaded it onto my truck. Then I went back inside the vault to get the other $100,000 for the smaller trunk. Johnny was just outside the door of the vault again. His job was to keep watch and load the trunk with the money as I handed it to him. When I tried to leave with the first batch of cash for the second trunk, the vault door was jammed and I couldn't get out. That's when I first smelled smoke. I thought Johnny and Daley had double-crossed me and trapped me in the vault. That made me mad. I pushed against the door as hard as I could, but it wouldn't budge, so I stepped back and got up a head of steam. I hit the door with my full force, and it flew open fast."

I thought I knew where this was going. "And when you got out, you killed Johnny?"

Sal's answer was nearly incomprehensible. "No. Not on purpose, but yes."

"Okay, so why don't you explain to me how you accidentally murdered him?"

"I'm trying!" Sal protested.

"Go on then."

"So Johnny was still right there on the other side of the vault door when I slammed into it. When the door flew open, it must have hit him hard on the head. It knocked him out cold. I tried to bring him around, but he was lights out. The smoke smell was getting strong and I knew the building was on fire. I heard footsteps of people coming toward us, and I thought I heard cops. I got scared. I put Johnny in the trunk so no one would notice him, and I dragged the trunk into the trash room around the corner. Then I went outside."

I was horrified. "You left him there to be burned alive?"

Sal started with the same ridiculous answer. "No. Not on purpose, but yes. I came back to get him as soon as I could after the people left. By the time I got back inside, the smoke was thick and the fire had gotten to the room where I'd put the trunk. Johnny was in bad shape, but he was still breathing, so I loaded him into my trailer. I was getting out when I heard the gunshots, so I ran to the front and climbed in the cab.

Sal must have been climbing in as I was crawling under. "And then what?"

"Then I drove back to my house and opened the trunk... but I was too late to save Johnny.

I didn't mean to, but I killed him. I told you D was to blame because he got us into this, but I'm to blame for Johnny being dead."

He certainly was. "Why didn't you just take him out to your truck in the first place?"

"I didn't know how bad the fire was, and I thought we could go back into the vault to get the rest of the money once Johnny was conscience again."

"It's conscious."

Sal furrowed his brow. "Huh?"

"Conscious is what you are when you *come to* after a guy knocks you out with a heavy vault door. Conscience is what should make the guy who knocked you out feel bad for doing that."

Tears were forming in Sal's eyes, but I had more questions. "Did Daley work at the El Rancho?"

"I guess so. He never said. I met him when I was gambling there one day."

"And he just casually asked you if you wanted to rob the place?"

"It wasn't like that," Sal insisted. "We started

hanging out there together, playing cards mostly, and he started telling me how he knew people who could help me get a better job... people with connections around town. It was a few months before he asked me about taking the money."

"And you asked Johnny to help?"

"Yeah. Johnny needed the cash. He gambled too much, and he was bad at it. He was in deep with the Silver Slipper, and they were threatening to fire him if he didn't pay back his marker. He thought about it for a while, but after talking with Daley, he said yes."

I grilled Sal on whether he ever saw Johnny cheating at cards or dice, and if he knew whether Johnny was familiar with Robert Schulze on a personal basis. His answer was no to both. I threw the rest of my B names at him, but nothing registered. He also said he didn't know if there was anyone else working above or with Mr. B. "And you didn't know about the plan to burn down the El Rancho?"

"I don't know if it even was a plan," he said. "If it was, no one told me. When I saw Daley before we got started, he was talking about a fire that happened there before, but he never said anything about starting one with Johnny and me inside. He smelled of booze, as usual, so I just figured it was nonsense. Maybe it was, I dunno. Maybe the fire was a coincidence. Like I told you, the first I knew of it was when I smelled smoke when I was inside the vault. I asked Daley about it later, and he just said he was done talking about that night. He said the less I knew the better it was for both of us."

I realized then that I might be alive today because Calvin Daley smelled of booze that night. Drunk men rarely have good aim. "What did you do with Johnny's body?"

"Daley took my truck and the trunk with Johnny in it the day after the fire," Sal said. "I don't know where he took Johnny, and that's the last time I saw Daley... until I found that picture when I went by the house a couple days ago."

"And the money?"

"I kept my cut and Johnny's too, and gave

the rest to Daley when he took Johnny's body. After Daley took his cut, there was only $140,000 left, not the $240,000 we were supposed to have for Mr. B. Daley said he would smooth things over." Sal pointed to the photo. "*That* doesn't look smoothed!"

I didn't see the point in telling Sal that things would likely have gone much smoother if he and Calvin Daley hadn't taken their full cut out of a short take. If Mr. B was expecting $240,000, he would not be happy with $140,000 and a burned up body. I asked Sal why he took Johnny's cut too, when Johnny was dead.

"I figure he earned it. We did the job they asked us to do, until the fire stopped us. I kept Johnny's money for his sister."

I was growing weary of the conversation… and wary of where it was headed. "Why are you here, Sal?"

"I want you to tell Jenny where to find the money. And if anyone ever comes looking for me, I want her to tell them that the same thing happened to me that happened to Calvin Daley. You tell them that too."

I wondered why Sal would think anyone would come to me asking about him. Then it hit me that he didn't know I hadn't been talking to anyone about what I knew from that night. I saw no reason to enlighten him. "So you're planning to skip town now I assume?"

"For a long time… as soon as I leave your office. If you let me go."

I wasn't sure I wanted to do that. I sensed that Sal was telling the truth, but he was responsible for what happened to Johnny, which was an awful thing. Then again, he had gone back in to try to help, at the expense of several of his digits. And Johnny wasn't exactly blameless himself… play with fire, you get burned, as they say.

I looked to Mae, and our shoulders went up together. I realized if I reported Sal and Johnny's part in what happened at the El Rancho, it could be even more dangerous for Jenny if someone thought she knew too much. It could be dangerous for me too, and I wasn't even sure anyone would believe my story if I did tell it.

I made my decision. I was placing Sal in my own Black Book. "You don't leave town for a long time, Sal... you leave town *forever*. You never set foot in Las Vegas again."

He didn't argue.

"And one more thing. Before you disappear, you take your cut of the money and you put it wherever you put Johnny's. You can keep one-way bus fare… that's it."

Sal nodded in agreement and handed me a piece of paper that showed where Jenny could find the cash. Then he stood up, gave a heavy sigh, and walked out the door without looking back.

CHAPTER TWENTY-NINE

The moment Sal Leonardo left is the moment I realized that the rest of this case would never be solved... not by me anyway, and I was the only one who was ever trying.

I had what I needed to know about what happened to Johnny and me the night of the El Rancho Vegas fire. I had the truck driver, the thief, and the accidental murderer. I had the shooter, the safecracker, and the possible arsonist. Sal's note had been wrong when it said I needed Mr. B. I *wanted* him, but I didn't *need* him. Even if I had needed him, with Johnny and Calvin Daley dead and Sal gone, Mr. B was a wild goose I could never catch.

Could Beldon Katleman have had any number of reasons to burn down his own casino just after he'd made sure the bulk of the money was saved? Could Bob Schulze have had any number of reasons to be involved with Johnny Ronson in cheating or robbery, or both?

Could Howard Hughes or Maurice Friedman have been acting on old grudges? Could Ben Aronoff have been acting on a more recent one? Could John Battaglia have been acting on behalf of his friend John Roselli or a mob family in Los Angeles or Chicago?

Could Benny Binion have been up to no good? Could Butch Leypoldt have gone bad?

And could Mr. B be sitting dead in Bert Engel's garage?

The answer to all of those questions was yes, they were all possible. But I had no hard evidence to tie any of the men to any activity that isn't commonplace in Las Vegas. Sal Leonardo had given me a confession to crimes that no one even knew existed, and I was the only one who had definitely done something wrong when I allowed him to go free and Jenny Ronson to profit from her brother Johnny's crimes.

Mae and I sat in silence. The expression on her face matched the feeling in my stomach. Eventually she telephoned Amy and told her everything. I finished pouring my scotch. I poured one for Mae too.

CHAPTER THIRTY

I opened my eyes Monday morning and looked at my bedside clock… 10:45. The phone rang a minute later, and it was Amy. She was coming over to make breakfast. She said Jenny got the money and was going back to Hawaii for a while, maybe permanently.

I left the bed long enough to retrieve my morning mail… a utility bill, the new issue of *LIFE*, and a thick envelope from my mother.

I climbed back under the covers and opened the envelope. I started to sift through the stack of clippings she'd sent, but I never made it past the first one. It was a short Associated Press story dated Thursday, June 16, 1960… one day *before* the El Rancho Vegas fire. I'd only been looking at newspapers from *after*.

The headline announced the settlement of the Katlemen/Aronoff lawsuit. They'd spelled Beldon's name wrong in the story, but it still started with a B. So did Benjamin's.

LAS VEGAS (AP) — Dist. Judge George Marshall decided Wednesday that Beldom Katleman owes Benjamin Aronoff $240,000 for a former interest in the El Rancho hotel casino.

I fell back into my pillow. The timing and the number were just more coincidences, right?

Maybe, maybe not, but this case was closed either way. The previous night's melancholy had already been replaced by merriment. Amy was on her way, and I didn't have to be out of bed again until 9 a.m. on Tuesday.

EPILOGUE

No one was ever charged with arson or any other crime in connection with the fire at the El Rancho Vegas, and the cause remains unknown to this day. The resort was never rebuilt, and the property has remained largely undeveloped and underused since June 17, 1960.

One year after the fire, W.E. "Butch" Leypoldt stepped down as Clark County Sheriff to take a position on the Nevada Gaming Commission.

In 1964, that same Commission shut down the Silver Slipper casino when shaved dice were discovered at one of the craps tables. The majority owner at the time was Robert O. "Bob" Schulze.

John Battaglia stayed in the Commission's Black Book until his death in 1975. Benny Binion was never in the book.

In 1967, six men, including Maurice Friedman and John Roselli were indicted for cheating at high stakes gin rummy card games. The games took place in the home of Beldon Katleman, who had moved to California not long after the fire.

Ben Aronoff went back to Ohio and was never again a part of any gambling operation in the state of Nevada.

Howard Hughes did return to Las Vegas, and when he came back, he bought the El Rancho property, along with both the Silver Slipper casino and the Frontier resort.

John “Jack” Kennedy was elected president, Sonny Liston won the title, Kirk Douglas lived to be 103, and Wayne Newton became known as Mr. Las Vegas… with a career that outlasted almost everyone and everything mentioned herein.

BRIAN WAYNE WEBER is a trademark attorney with a long-standing interest in Las Vegas casino history and memorabilia. Like Beldon Katleman, Brian was born in Iowa. Brian's biggest Las Vegas regret is that on his first trip to the city as a young adult, he chose an ice skating show over seeing Redd Foxx at the Hacienda.

Brian currently lives near the Las Vegas Strip, directly west of the El Rancho Vegas property, on land that was once part of the ranch owned by Michael and Ingrid (Braecklein) Hines.

Fire and Fate in Vegas is Brian's first work of historical fiction.

Website: FireAndFate.com

Contact: fireandfateinvegas@gmail.com

DEDICATION, ACKNOWLEDGMENTS, AND CREDITS

This book is dedicated to Emely Gonzalez, Kris Kesterson, and Janice Weber.

To Emely, for taking a chance and moving with me to Las Vegas, and for your picture that is worth 25,000 of my words. You were the first person to see this story, and you made it better, just as you make me better.

To Kris, for being my lifelong Marty Grimball. Your research basically wrote the plot for Part Two, and your constant motivation made me realize I could do this. (Kris is the author of many books, including Coach: Maury John's Journey to the Pinnacle of College Hoops).

And to my mom, Janice Weber, for the support you've always given me, and for reading the same words over and over again, as often as I asked you to... until I was confident that I got them right.

My thanks to other family members and friends, including Diana Cruz, Camille Boyette, and my sister, Stacey Shriner, for reading drafts; also Noemi Garcia, Henry Cruz, Sam Shriner, and my dad, Wayne Weber, for helping me pick the cover.

My sincere appreciation to the many terrific people who made significant contributions to this project. In particular, to Caroline Teagle Johnson of HarperCollins and Reedsy.com, for a design that far exceeded my expectations for how reminiscent of the vintage style this book could be. I feel lucky to have benefitted from your incredible talent. And to Lynn M. Zook, author of Gambling on a Dream: The Classic Las Vegas Strip 1930-1955, for sharing your vast knowledge of Las Vegas history, and for your website and blog at ClassicLasVegas.com, which inspired me to further develop my own appreciation of the city's amazing past.

To Chris Hines, for your keen editing eye, and for the stories of your parents and the Hines Ranch, which gave me two of my favorite paragraphs; to Channing Reagan and Deanna Harkess Reagan, for the fantastic background information about your family's bakery; and to Stan Armstrong of Desert Rose Productions, for so many great details about West Las Vegas that I'd need to write ten books to include them all, and for letting me include your dad.

To Susan Agaman, John Maggio, Paul Costanzo, and many other eBay sellers, for offering up a treasure trove of artifacts that provided period-specific details I couldn't have found anywhere else; and to Hubert Yanez of the Golden Steer Steakhouse, Brent Bell of Whittlesea Blue Cab, and Luis Monda of Johnny Tocco's Ringside Gym, for the historical information about these businesses... all of which are still around today!

To Su Kim Chung and the Special Collections and Archives library at UNLV, Terry Shaffer (author of Illegal Gambling Clubs of Toledo), Richard Mondio at PlanetXV.com, the Las Vegas-Clark County Library District,

The Neon Museum's Education Department, and the Nevada State Museum, for offering feedback, providing resources, answering questions, and/or referring me to people who could.

Credit to LunaPic.com and Freepik.com for online design resources that helped create the note images; to the Las Vegas Review-Journal, Rebecca Clifford-Cruz and the Las Vegas Sun, Sean Scully and the Napa Valley Register, and the Associated Press, for allowing free or reasonably priced use of article and headline excerpts... with special recognition to Tricia Gesner at the Associated Press for being extraordinarily responsive; and to the family of Hal Rothman, for being so gracious in allowing me to use a quote from his excellent work, Neon Metropolis, to set the mood for this story.

And finally, thank you to whoever wrote the statement below, for words that encouraged me to try to capture the essence of what made Las Vegas unique way back when.

Americans like to gamble, and as long as Las Vegas lasts they won't have the slightest difficulty getting a little action – with girls, comedians, crooners, attractive hotel rates, sun, A-bombs, jet planes, and a dam named Hoover to boot.

—International News Service, 1955

I'm grateful to you all.
Brian

Made in the USA
Columbia, SC
20 February 2023

12703353R00119